FISHING THE

SLOE-BLACK RIVER

FISHING THE

SLOE-BLACK RIVER

Stories

COLUM McCANN

PICADOR
A METROPOLITAN BOOK
HENRY HOLT AND COMPANY
NEW YORK

www.picadorusa.com

Picador® is a U.S. registered trademark and is used by Henry Holt and Company under license from Pan Books Limited.

For information on Picador Reading Group Guides, as well as ordering, please contact the Trade Marketing department at St. Martin's Press.
Phone: 1-800-221-7945 extension 763
Fax: 212-677-7456
E-mail: trademarketing@stmartins.com

Designed by Jessica Shatan

Library of Congress Cataloging-in-Publication Data

McCann, Colum, 1965–
    Fishing the sloe-black river : stories / Colum McCann.
        p. cm.
    ISBN 0-312-42338-1
    1. Ireland—Social life and customs—Fiction. 2. Irish Americans—Social life and customs—Fiction. I. Title.

PR6063.C335F57 1996
823'.914—dc20

96-19779
CIP

First published in the United Kingdom by Phoenix House

First published in the United States by Metropolitan Books, an imprint of Henry Holt and Company

First Picador Edition: February 2004

For my father and mother.
And for Roger and Rose Marie

CONTENTS

SISTERS

I have come to think of our lives as the colors of that place—
hers a piece of bog cotton, mine as black as the water found
when men slash too deep in the soil with a shovel.

I remember when I was fifteen, cycling across those bogs in
the early evenings, on my way to the dancehall in my clean,
yellow socks. My sister stayed at home. I tried to avoid puddles,
but there would always be a splash or two on the hem of my
dress. The boys at the dancehall wore blue anoraks and watched
me when I danced. Outside they leaned against my bike and
smoked shared cigarettes in the night. I gave myself. One of
them once left an Easter lily in the basket. Later it was men in
granite-gray suits who would lean into me, heads cocked sideways like hawks, eyes closed. Sometimes I would hold my
hands out beyond their shoulders and shape or carve something
out of my fingers, something with eyes and a face, someone
very little, within my hand, whose job it was to try to understand. Between a statue of Our Lady and a Celtic cross com-

memorating the dead of Ireland, my hand made out the shape of a question mark as a farm boy furrowed his way inside me.

A man with a walrus mustache gone gray at the tips took me down to the public lavatories in Castlebar. He was a sailor. He smelled of ropes and disuse and seaport harridans. There were bays and coverts, hillsides and heather. My promiscuity was my autograph. I was hourglassy, had turf-colored hair and eyes as green as wine bottles. Someone once bought me an ice-cream in Achill Island, then we chipped some amethyst out of the rock banks and climbed the radio tower. We woke up late at the edge of a cliff, with the waves lashing in from the Atlantic. There was a moon of white reflected in the water. The next day at the dinner table, my father told us that John F. Kennedy had landed a man on the moon. We knew that Kennedy was long dead—he stared at us from a picture frame on the wall—but we said nothing. It was a shame, my father said, looking at me, that the moon turned out to be a heap of ash.

My legs were stronger now, and I strolled to the dancehall, the bogs around me wet and dark. The boy with the Easter lily did it again, this time with nasturtiums stolen from outside the police station. My body continued to go out and around in all the right places. My father waited up for me, smoking Woodbines down to the quick. He told me once that he had overheard a man at his printing shop call me "a wee whore," and I heard him weeping as I tuned in Radio Luxembourg in my room.

My older sister, Brigid, succeeded with a spectacular anorexia. After classes she would sidle off to the bog, to a large rock where she thought nobody could see her, her Bible in her pocket, her sandwiches in her hand. There she would perch like a raked robin, and bit by bit she would tear up the bread like a sacrament and throw it all around her. The rock had a history—in penal times it had been used as a meeting place for mass. I sometimes watched her from a distance. She was a house of bones, my sister, throwing her bread away. Once, out on the rock, I saw her take my father's pliers to her fingers and slowly pluck out the nail from the middle finger of her left hand. She did it because she had heard that the Cromwellians had done it to harpists in the seventeenth century, so they could no longer pluck the cat-gut to make music. She wanted to know how it felt. Her finger bled for days. She told our father that she had caught her hand in a school door. He stayed unaware of Brigid's condition, still caught in the oblivion caused, many years before, by the death of our mother—lifted from a cliff by a light wind while out strolling. Since that day Brigid had lived a strange sort of martyrdom. People loved her frail whiteness but never really knew what was going on under all those sweaters. She never went to the dancehall. Naturally, she wore the brown school socks that the nuns made obligatory. Her legs within them were thin as twigs. We seldom talked. I never tried. I envied her that unused body that needed so little, yet I also loved her with a bitterness that only sisters can have.

Now, two decades later, squashed in the boot of a car, huddled under a blanket, I ask myself why I am smuggling myself across the Canadian border to go back to a country that wouldn't allow me to stay, to see a sister I never really knew in the first place.

It is dark and cramped and hollow and black in here. My knees are up against my breasts. Exhaust fumes make me cough. A cold wind whistles in. We are probably still in the country-side of Quebec. At every traffic light I hope that this is the border station leading into Maine. Perhaps when we're finally across we can stop by a frozen lake and skim out there on the ice, Michael and I.

When I asked Michael to help smuggle me across the border he didn't hesitate. He liked the idea of being what the Mexicans call a "coyote." He said it goes with his Navajo blood, his forefathers believing that coyotes howled in the beginning of the universe. Knowing the reputation of my youth, he joked that I could never have believed in that legend, that I must go in for the Big Bang. In the boot of the car I shudder in the cold. I wear a blue wool hat pulled down over my ears. My body does not sandwich up the way it used to.

I met Michael on a Greyhound bus in the early seventies, not long after leaving the bogs. I had left Brigid at home with her untouched platefuls of food. At Shannon Airport my father had cradled me like his last cigarette. On the plane I realized that I was gone forever to a new country—I was tired of the knowing way women back home nodded their heads at me. I was on my way to San Francisco, wearing a string of beads. In the bus station at Port Authority I noticed Michael first for his menac-ing darkness; his skin looked like it had been dipped in hot

4

molasses. And then I saw the necklace of teeth that hung on his chest. I learned later that they were the teeth of a mountain lion. He had found the lion one afternoon in the Idaho wilderness, the victim of a road kill. Michael came over and sat beside me, saying nothing, smelling faintly of woodsmoke. His face was aquiline, acned. His wrists were thick. He wore a leather waistcoat, jeans, boots. On the bus I leaned my head on his shoulder, feigning sleep. Later my hand reached over and played with the necklace of teeth. He laughed when I blew on them. I said they sounded like wind chimes, tinkling together, though they didn't sound anything like that at all. We rattled across a huge America. I lived with him for many years, in San Francisco on Dolores Street near the Mission, the foghorn of the Golden Gate keening a lament. After the raid, in 1978, when I was gone and home in Ireland, I would never again sleep with another man.

The car shudders to a halt. My head lolls against the lid of the boot. I would rather pick my way through a pillar of stone with a pin than go through this again. There is a huge illegal trade going on with cigarettes and alcohol crossing the border. We could be stopped. Michael wanted to take me across by paddling a canoe down the Kennebec River, but I said I would rather just do it in the car. Now I wish we'd done it his way. "Up a lazy river with a robin song, it's a lazy, lazy river we can float along, blue skies up above, everyone's in love." My father had sung that when Brigid and I were young.

Slowly the car pitches forward. I wonder whether we are finally there or whether this is just another traffic light along the way. We stop again and then we inch up. I ask myself what plays in Michael's head. I was shocked when I saw him first, just three days ago, because he still looked much the same after thirteen years. I was ashamed of myself. I felt dowdy and gray. When I went to sleep on his sofabed, alone, I remembered the new creases on the backs of my thighs. Now I feel more his equal. He has cut his hair and put on a suit to lessen the risk of being caught—giving him some of the years that I have gained, or lost, I don't know which.

A muffle of voices. I curl myself even deeper into a ball and press my face against the cold metal. If the border patrol asks to examine his luggage, I am gone again, history come full circle. But I hear the sound of a hand slapping twice on the roof of the car, a grind of gears, a jolt forward, and within moments we are in America, the country, as someone once said, that God gave to Cain. A few minutes down the road I hear Michael whoop and roar and laugh.

"Greetings," he shouts, "from the sebaceous glands. I'm sweating like a bear. I'll have you out of there in no time, Sheona."

His voice sounds smothered and my toes are frozen.

On an August night in 1978 I clocked off my job as a singing waitress in a bar down on Geary Street. Wearing an old wedding dress I had bought in a pawn shop, hair let loose, yellow socks on—they were always my trademark—I got into our old Ford pickup with the purple hubcaps and drove up the coast. Michael was spending the weekend in a cabin somewhere north of Mendocino, helping bring in a crop of California's

6

best. Across the bridge where the hell-divers swooped, into Sausalito, around by Mount Tamalpais, where I flung a few cigarette butts to the wind for the ghosts of Jack Kerouac and John Muir, and up along the coast, the sun rose like a dirty red aspirin over the sea. I kept steady to the white lines, those on the dashboard and those on the road. The morning had cracked well when I turned up the Russian River and followed the directions Michael had written on the back of a dollar bill.

The cabin was up a drunken mountain road. Cats leaped among parts of old motorbikes, straggles of orange crates, pieces of a windmill. Tatters of wild berries hung on bushes, and sunlight streamed in shafts between the sequoias. Michael and his friends met me with guns slung down at their waists. There had been no guns in Mayo, just schoolgirl rumors of an IRA man who lived in a boghole about a mile from Brigid's rock. They scared me, the guns. I asked Michael to tuck his away. Late that evening, when all the others had gone with a truck-load of dope, I asked him if we could spend a moment together. I wanted to get away from the guns. I didn't get away from them for long, though. Four hours later, naked on the side of a creek, I was quoting Kavanagh for some reason, my own love banks green and rampant with leaves, when I looked up beyond Michael's shoulder at four cops, guns cocked, laughing. They forced Michael to bend over and shoved a tree branch up his anus. They tried to take me, these new hawks, and eventually they did. Four in a row. This time with my eyes closed, hands to the ground and nothing to watch me from my fingerhouse.

Five days later, taking the simple way out—a lean, young lawyer in a white fedora had begun to take an interest in my case—they deported me for not having a green card. Past the Beniano Bufano Peace statue—the mosaic face of all races—at San Francisco International, handcuffed, they escorted me to JFK on to an Aer Lingus Boeing 747. I flung my beads down the toilet.

Michael lifts me from the boot. He swirls me around in his arms, in the middle of a Maine dirt road. It is pitch black but I can almost smell the lakes and the fir trees, the clean snow that nestles upon branches. A winter Orion thrusts his sword after Taurus in the sky. "That could be a ghost," I whisper to Michael, and he stops his dance. "I mean, the light hitting our eyes from those stars left millions of years ago. It just might be that the thing is a ghost, already imploded. A supernova."

"The only thing I know about the stars is that they come out at night," he says. "My grandfather sometimes sat in a chair outside our house and compared them to my grandmother's teeth."

I laugh and lean into him. He looks up at the sky.

"Teach me some more scientific wonders," he says.

I babble about the notion that if we could travel faster than the speed of light we would get to a place we never really wanted to go before we even left. He looks at me quizzically, puts his fingers on my lips, walks me to the car and sits me down gently on the front seat, saying, "Your sister."

He takes off his tie, wraps it around his head like a bandanna, feels for a moment for his gone ponytail, turns up the stereo, and we drive toward New York.

I had seen my sister one day in Dublin, outside the Dawson Lounge. I suppose her new convent clothes suited her well. Black to hide the thinness. Muttering prayers as she walked. The hair had grown thick on her hands, and her cheekbones were sculleried away in her head. I followed behind her, up around St. Stephen's Green and on down toward the Dail. She shuffled her feet slowly, never lifting them very high off the ground. She stopped at the gate of the Dail, where a group of homeless families sat protesting their destitution, flapping their arms like hummingbirds to keep themselves warm. It was Christmas Eve. She talked with a few of them for a moment, then took out a blanket and sat down among them. I looked from the other side of the street. It shocked me to see her laugh and to watch a small girl leap into her lap. I walked away, bought a loaf of bread, and threw it to the ducks in the Green. A boy in Doc Martens glared at me and I thought of the dancehall.

"None of these coins have our birthdates on them anymore," I say as I search in my handbag for some money for a toll booth.

"I enjoyed that back there," he says. "Hell of a lot better than being on a scaffold. Hey, you should have seen the face of the border patrol guy. Waved me through without batting an eyelid."

"You think we just get older and then we fade away?"

"Look, Sheona, you know the saying."

"What saying?"

"A woman is as old as she feels." Then he chuckles. "And a man is as old as the woman he feels."

"Very funny."

"I'm only kidding," he says.

"I'm sorry, Mike. I'm just nervous."

I lean back in the seat and watch him. In the six years of notes he sent from prison there is one I remember the most. "I wouldn't mind dying in the desert with you, Sheona," he had written. "We could both lick the dew off the rocks, then watch the sun and let it blind us. Dig a hole and piss in the soil. Put a tin can in the bottom of the hole. Cover it with a piece of plastic and weigh down the center with a rock. The sun'll evaporate the piss, purify it, let it gather in droplets on the plastic, where it'll run toward the center, then drop in the tin can, making water. After a day we can drink from each other's bodies. And then die well. Let the buzzards come down from the thermals. I hate being away from you. I am dead already."

The day I received that letter, I thought of quitting my secretarial job in a glass tower down by Kavanagh's canals. I thought of going back to Mayo and striking a shovel into a boghole, seeping down into the water, breathing out the rest of my life through a hollow piece of reed grass. But I never quit my job and I never wrote back to him. The thought of that sort of death was way too beautiful.

My days in Dublin were derelict and ordinary. A flat on Appian Way near enough to Raglan Road, where my own dark hair weaved a snare. Thirteen years somehow slipped away, like they do, not even autumn foliage now, but mulched delicately into my skin. I watched unseen as a road sweeper in Temple Bar whistled like he had a bird in his throat. I began to notice cranes swinging across the skyline. Dublin had become cosmopolitan. A drug addict in a doorway on Leeson Street ferreted in his bowels for a small bag of cocaine. Young boys wore baseball hats. The canals carried fabulously colored litter. The postman asked me if I was lonely. I went to Torremolinos in 1985 and watched girls my age get knocked up in alleyways.

But I didn't miss the men. I bought saucepans, cooked beautiful food, wrote poems near a single bar electric heater. Once I even went out with a policeman from Donegal, but when he lifted my skirt I knocked his glasses off. At work, in a ribboned blouse, I was so unhappy that I couldn't even switch jobs. When making calls, I was always breaking my fingernails on the phone slots. I watched a harpist in the Concert Hall playing beautifully on nylon strings. In a moment of daring I tried to find my sister exactly two years to the day that I had seen her, huddled with the homeless in a Foxford blanket. "Sister Brigid," I was told, "is spreading the word of God in Central America." I didn't have the nerve to ask for the address. All I knew of Central America was dogs leaner than her.

We are off the highway now, looking for a New Hampshire petrol station. The sun in the east is bleeding into the darkness. Michael refuses to fill up at the garages that lick the big interstate. He prefers a smaller town. He's still the same man, now wearing his necklace of mountain lion teeth over an open-necked Oxford. Because I trust him, because he still believes in simpler, more honest things, I tell him about why I think Brigid is sick. I am very simple in my ideas of Central America. My information comes from newspapers. She is sick, I tell him, because she was heartbroken among the maguey plants. She is sick because there are soldiers on the outskirts of town who carry Kalashnikovs or AK-47's, hammering the barrels through the brick kilns that make the dough rise. She is sick because she saw things that she thought belonged only in Irish history. She is sick because she saw girls bonier than her and because there was no such thing as a miracle to be found. She is sick, she is in an infirmary convent on Long Island for nuns who have or have not done their jobs. Though really, honestly, I think she is sick because she knew I was watching when she flung her bread from a rock and I never said a word.

"You're too hard on yourself," says Michael.

"I've been picking my way through a pillar of stone with a pin."

"What does that mean?"

"Oh come on, Michael, it's not as if we're twenty-one any more. All those years spat away."

"It doesn't help to be bitter," he says.

"Oh, and you're not bitter?"

"I've learned not to think about it."

"That's worse than being bitter, Michael."

"Come on," he says, reaching across to take my hand. "You can't change the past."

"No we can't," I say. My hand is limp. "We can't, can we?"

Embarrassed at my anger, I tell him once again, for the ump-teenth time over the last three days, about how I found out where she was. I decided, only a week ago, to go back and see my father. I brought him a carton of Major because I couldn't find Woodbines. I have no idea what stirred me to see him, except that one of the other secretaries in Dublin had talked all morning long about her pet collie dog throwing up over her favorite rug. She was actually weeping over it, more for the rug, I imagine, than for the dog. I walked out to the canal and sat watching boys diving in, breaking up the oily slime. Their recklessness astounded me. I went to Heuston station and took a train west.

He was dead, of course. The couple who had bought our old bungalow had three babies now. They said they had been with my father in a hospital in Galway when, in an oxygen tent, he asked for a nip of Bushmill's and a smoke. The doctors had told him that he would explode and he had said, "That's grand, give me a smoke, so." The husband asked who I was even though he knew exactly who I was. I didn't want him to bring out nasturtiums or Easter lilies. I told him, in front of his wife, that I was a distant cousin. In a whisper, at the gate, he told me he had heard that Brigid was sick and was living now in a convent in the "Big Apple." He stole a furtive kiss on my cheek. I wiped it off in disgust, went home to Dublin and made phone calls until I found Michael living in Quebec, a foreman at a building site.

"Michael, I need to get back in. I can get a flight from London into Canada, no hassle."

"I'll pick you up at the airport in Montreal."

"Are you married?" I asked.

"Are you kidding? Are you?"

"Are you kidding?" I laughed. "Will you take me there?"

"Yeah."

It's one highway, 95, all the way, a torrent of petrol stations, neon signs, motels, fast-food spires. Michael talks of a different world beyond this, where in his boredom he watched the sun fall and rise and fall again. San Quentin had taught him about looking out windows. The day he got out, in a suit two sizes too big, he learned how to cartwheel again and ended up tearing the polyester knees. He took a bus to Yosemite and got a job as a guide. He took a motorbike, a "rice burner" he called it, from California to Gallup, New Mexico, where his mother and father pissed away a monthly government check into a dry creekbed at the back of their house. Michael slept in a shed full of Thunderbird bottles, a hole in the corrugated ceiling where he watched the stars, bitterly charting their roll across the sky. He followed them east. He climbed scaffolds to build New York City high-rises. Navaho and Mohawk climbers were in big demand for that type of job and the money was good.

Then there was a girl. She brought him to Quebec. They climbed frozen waterfalls in a northern forest. The girl was long gone, but the waterfalls weren't. Maybe, he says, when we get back to Quebec he'll put me in a harness and spiked boots and we'll go scaling. I finger my thighs and say perhaps.

Floods of neon rush by.

We stop in a diner and a trucker offers Michael ten dollars for the lion-tooth necklace. Michael tells him that it's a family heirloom and then, trying to make sure that I don't hear—me, in my red crocheted cardigan and gray skirt—the trucker offers him a bag full of pills. Michael still has that sort of face. It's been years since I've been wired, and I have a faint urge to drop some pills. But Michael thanks the trucker, says that he hasn't done speed in years and we drive away.

By late evening the next day, we snarl into the New York City traffic and head down toward the Village. Michael's eyes are creased and tired. The car is littered with coffee cups and the smell of cigarettes lingers in our clothes. The city is much like any other to me now, a clog of people and cars. It seems appropriate that there is no room for us in the Chelsea Hotel, no more Dylan, no more Behan, no more Cohen remembering us well. Old songs flow through me as we drive away. We stay with a friend of Michael's on Bleecker Street. I have brought two nightdresses in my suitcase. My greatest daring is that I don't wear either of them. Michael and his friend curl on the ends of the sofa. I sleep in a bed, scared of the sheets. Four red-beaked hawks in badges grunting down from the thermals by a gentle creek in sequoia sunlight. A bouquet of boys shimmy in from the bogs in brown tweed hats and pants tucked in with silver bicycle clips. My father lights a carton of cigarettes and burns in a plastic tent. A nun runs around with dough rising up in her belly. My wrists pinned to pine needles, no light wind to carry me away. Blood running down the backs of his thighs.

The talons of a robin carrying off flowers. I toss and turn in sweat that gathers in folds and it is not until Michael comes over and kisses my eyelids that I find sleep.

On the drive out to Long Island I buy a bunch of daffodils from a street vendor. He tells me that daffodils mean marriage. I tell him that they're for a nun. He tugs at his hat. "You never know, hon," he says, "you never know these days."

Michael still gropes for the back of his hair as he drives, and every now and then he squeezes my forearm and says it'll be all right. The expressway is a vomit of cars but gradually, as we move, the traffic thins out and the pace quickens. Occasional flecks of snow get tossed away by the windshield wipers. I curl into a shell and listen to the sound of what might be waves. I am older now. I have no right to be afraid. I think about plucking the petals from the flowers, one by one. We drive toward the ocean. Far off I can see gulls arguing over the waves.

The convent at Bluepoint looks like a school. There seems to be little holy about the place except for the statue of Our Lady on the front lawn, a coat of snow on her shoulders. We park the car and I ask Michael to wait. From under his shirt collar I flick out the necklace of teeth and, for the first time since I've seen him, kiss him flush on the lips. "Go on," he says, "don't be getting soppy on me now. And don't stay too long. Those waterfalls in Quebec melt very quickly."

He turns the radio up full blast and I walk toward the front entrance. Hold. Buckle. Swallow. The words of a poet who should have known: "What I do is me. For that I came." I rasp my fingers along the wood but it takes a long time for the heavy door to swing open.

"Yes dear?" says the old nun. She is Irish too, her face creased into dun and purple lines.

"I'd like to see Brigid O'Dwyer."

She looks at me, scans my face. "No visitors, I'm sorry," she says. "Sister Brigid needs just a wee bit of peace and quiet." She begins to close the door, smiling gently at me.

"Is mise a dhreifeur," I stutter. I am her sister.

The door opens again and she looks at me, askance.

"Bhfuil tú cinnte?" Are you sure?

"Sea," I laugh. "Táim cinnte." Yes, I'm sure.

"Cad a bhfuil uait?" she asks. What do you want?

"I want to see her. Sé do thoil é. Please."

She stares at me for a long time. "Tar isteach. Come in, girl." She takes the daffodils and touches my cheek. "You have her eyes."

I move into the corridor where some other old nuns gather like moss, asking questions. "She's very sick," says one. "She won't be seeing anyone." The nun who met me at the door shuffles away. There are flowers by the doorway, paintings on the walls, a smell of potpourri, a quality of whiteness flooding all the colors. I sit in a steel chair with my knees nailed together, my hands in my lap, watching their faces, hearing the somber chatter, not responding. A statue of the Madonna stares at me. I am a teenager now in a brown convent skirt. It is winter. After camogie, in the school showers, one or two of the nuns stand around and watch my classmates and me as we wash the dirt off our legs. They see bruises on my inner thigh and then they tell me about Magdalene. I ride away from the school gates. I flagrantly pedal my bicycle with my skirt up high. I see her there, on the rock, sucking her finger, making a cross of reeds, the emblem of the saint for whom she was named. My father puts some peat on the fire. That's grand, give me a smoke, so.

"Will you join us for a cup? She's sleeping now." It's the old nun who answered the door.

"Thank you, Sister."

"You look white, dear."

"I've been traveling a long time."

Over tea and scones they begin to melt, these women. They surprise me with their cackle and their smiles. They ask of the old place. Brigid, they say. What a character. Was she always like that? The holy spirit up to the ears?

Two nuns there had spent the last few years with her. They tell me that she had been living in El Salvador in a convent outside a coffee plantation. One day recently three other nuns in the convent were shot, one of them almost fatally, so Brigid slipped out to a mountain for a few hours to pray for their health. She was found three days later, sitting on a rock. They look at me curiously when I ask about her fingernails. No, they say, her fingernails were fine. It was the lack of food that did it to her. Five campesinos had carried her down from the mountain. She was a favorite among the locals. She had always taken food to the women in the adobe houses, and the men respected her for the way she had hidden it under her clothes, so they wouldn't be shamed by charity. She'd spent a couple of weeks in a hospital in San Salvador, on an intravenous drip, then they transported her to Long Island to recover. She had never talked of any brothers or sisters, though she had gotten letters from Ireland. She did some of the strangest things in Central America, however. She carried a pebble in her mouth. It came all the way from the Sargasso Sea. She learned how to dance. She reared four piglets behind the sacristy in the local church. She had shown people how to skin rabbits. The pebble made little chips in her teeth. She had taken to wearing some very strange colored socks.

I start to laugh.

"Everyone," says one of the nuns with a Spanish accent, "is allowed a little bit of madness, even if you're a nun. I don't see what's wrong with that."

"No, no, no, there's nothing wrong with it. I'm just thinking."

"It does get cold down there, you know," she replies.

Someone talks about the time she burned the pinto beans. The time the pigs got loose from the pen. The time the rabbit ran away from her. Another says she once dropped a piece of cake from her dress when she knelt at the altar, and one of the priests, from Wales, said that God gave his only begotten bun. But the priest was forgiven for the joke since he was not a blasphemer, just a bit of a clown. The gardener comes in, a man from Sligo, and says: "I've seen more fat on a butcher's knife than I have on your sister." I leave the scone raisins on the side of the saucer. I am still laughing.

"Can I see her?" I say, turning to the nun who opened the door for me. "I really need to see her. I have a friend waiting for me outside and I must go soon."

The nun shuffles off to the kitchen. I wait. I think of a piece of turf and the way it holds so much history. I should have brought my sister a sod of soil. Or a rock. Or something.

An old nun, with an African accent, singing a hymn, comes out of the kitchen, carrying a piece of toast and a glass of water. She has put a dollop of jam on the side of a white plate, "for a special occasion." She winks at me and tells me to follow her. I feel eyes on my back, then a hum of voices as we leave the dining area. She leads me up the stairs, past a statue, eerie and white, down a long clean corridor, toward a room with a picture of Archbishop Romero on the door. We stop. I hold my breath. A piece of turf. A rock. Anything.

"Go in, child." The nun squeezes my hand. "You're shaking."

"Thank you," I say. I stand at the door and open it slowly. "Brigid?" The bedclothes are crumpled as if they've just been tossed. "Brigid. It's me. Sheona."

There's no sound, just a tiny hint of movement in the bedsheets. I walk over. Her eyes are open, but she's not there inside them. Her hair is netted and gray. The lines on her face cut inward. Age has assaulted her cheekbones. I feel angry. I take down the picture of the Sacred Heart that is spraying red light out into the room and place it face-down on the floor. She murmurs and a little spittle comes out the side of her mouth. So she is there, after all. I look in her eyes again. This is the first time I have seen her since we were still that age. A bitterness in there now, perhaps, borne deep. "I just want some neutral ground," I say. Then I realize that I don't know who I'm talking to, and I put the picture back on the wall.

I sit on the bed and touch her ashtrayed hair. "Talk to me," I say. She turns slightly. The toast is growing cold on a plate on the floor. I have no idea if she knows who I am as I feed her, but I have a feeling she does. I'm afraid to lay my hand on her for fear of snapping bones. She doesn't want to be fed. She hisses and spits the bread out of dehydrated lips. She closes her mouth on my fingers, but it takes no effort to pry it open. Her teeth are as brittle as chalk. I lay the toast on her tongue again. Each time it gets moister and eventually it dissolves. I wash it down with some water. I try to say something but I can't, so I sing a Hoagy Carmichael tune, but she doesn't acknowledge it. If I tried to lift her, I think I would find a heap of dust in my hand, my own hand, which is speaking to me again, carving out a moving shape.

I want to find out who is under the bedsheets. "Talk to me." She rolls away and turns her back to me. I stand and look around the room. It all comes down to a lump in the bed. An empty chamber pot. Some full-bloom chrysanthemums by the window. A white plate with a smear of jam. A dead archbishop on the outside, looking in.

"Just a single word," I say. "Just give me a single word."

Some voices float in from the white corridor. Frantic, I move to a set of drawers and a cupboard to look at the bits and pieces that go to make up Brigid now. I pull the drawers out and dump the contents on the floor. I cannot understand the mosaic. A bible. Some neatly folded blouses. Long underwear. A bundle of letters in an elastic band. Lots of hairpins. Stamps gleaned from the Book of Kells. Letters. I do not want to read them. A painting of a man sowing seeds, by a child's hand. A photograph of our mother and father, from a long time ago, standing together by Nelson's Pillar, him with a cigar, her with netting hanging down from her hat. A copy of a newspaper from a recent election. A Mayan doll. Lotus-legged on the floor, I am disappointed with the clutter of somebody else's life. I haven't found what I'm looking for.

I shuffle to the end of the bed and lift the sheets. Her feet are blue and very cold to the touch. I rub them slowly at first. I remember when we were children, very young, before all that, and we had held buttercups to each other's chins on the edges of brown fields. I want her feet to tell me that she remembers. As I massage I think I see her lean her head sideways and smile, though I'm not sure. I don't know why, but I want to take her feet in my mouth. I want to, but it seems obscene, so I don't. "Up a lazy river with a robin song, it's a lazy, lazy river, we can float along, blue skies up above, everyone's in love, up a lazy river with me." She mumbles when I lean over her face and kiss her. There is spittle on her chin and she is horribly ruined.

I walk to the window. Far off, in the parking lot, I can see Michael, head slumped forward on the steering wheel, sleeping. Two nuns look at him through the passenger window, curious, a cup of tea and some scones in their hands. I watch him too, wondering about the last few days. There's an old feeling within me that's new now. Those teeth around his neck. I want a bicycle again. Sequoia seedlings in the basket. I want to ride through a flurry of puddles to a place where a waterfall is frozen. I will stay here for now. I know that. But when she recovers, I will go to Quebec and climb.

But there is something I need first. I smile, go away from the window, lean towards Brigid, and whisper: "Where, Sister, did you put those yellow socks of mine anyway?"

BREAKFAST FOR

ENRIQUE

The only older men I know are the ones who rise early to work. They fish the ocean for sea trout and haddock, flaring out their boats from the wharf before the sun, coming back by mid-morning with huge white plastic barrels full of fish, ready for us to gut. They draw hard on unfiltered cigarettes and have big hands that run through mottled beards. Even the younger ones look old, the hair thinning, the eyes seaward. You can see them move, slow and gull-like, back to their boats when their catch has been weighed, stomping around in a mess of nets and ropes. They don't talk to the fishgutters. They hand us a sort of disdain, a quiet disregard, I believe, for the thinness of our forearms.

I think of them always in the mornings, when the light comes in through my curtains. The light is like an old fisherman in a yellow rain-slicked coat, come to look at Enrique and me, wrapped in our bedsheets.

It's a strange light that comes this morning, older, thicker-wristed, pushing its way through the gap and lying, with its smotes of dust, on the headboard. *Goddamn it, aren't you two just the salt of the earth?* Enrique is curled into himself, the curve of his back full against the spindle of his legs. His hair is all about his face. Stubbled hairs in a riot on his chin. His eyes have collected black bags, and his white T-shirt still has smatterings of spaghetti sauce from yesterday's lunch. I move to brush my lips against his cheek. Enrique stirs a little, and I notice a little necklace of blood spots on the pillow where he has been coughing. *Get up out of bed, you lazy shits.* I smooth Enrique's brow where the sweat has gathered, even in sleep.

I climb naked out of bed, swinging my feet down into my slippers. The floor is cold and I step carefully. Last night I smashed the blackberry jamjar that used to hold our money. The glass splayed in bright splinters all around the room. I move over to the window, and Enrique murmurs into the pillow. The curtains make the sound of crackling ice. The ghosts of old fishermen can tumble in here in droves now if they want, spit their epithets all around the room. *What the hell sort of mess is this? You're late for work, Paddy-boy. No foghorns going off this morning. Gut the fish along the side, asshole.*

Our window looks out to a steep hill of parked cars. This morning they are bumper to bumper. Drivers have turned their steering wheels sideways so their vehicles won't roll down the hill and fling themselves toward the sea. Two weeks ago Enrique and I sold our car for $2,700 to a man with lemon-colored hair, and all the money is gone already. Bags of medicine and a little bit of cocaine. I put our last line on his belly last night, but he was sweating so hard that it was almost impossible to snort it.

I look up the road toward the deli. The white light in the street is slouching on the buildings, spilling over the ironwork railings. What I like most about the street is that people put flower pots in their windows, a colorful daub of Mediterranean greens and reds. Doors are painted in a medley of shades. Curtains get thrown open early in the mornings. There's a cat on the third floor across the street, jet black with a dappled blue bandanna. It is forever cocking its head sideways and yawning in the window. Sometimes I bring home some sea trout and leave it on the doorstep of the house for the owner.

I cover myself with my hand and step out through the French doors. A chill wind is coming up from the waterfront, carrying the smell of salt water and fresh sourdough. Already some of the fishermen will have unloaded their catch and Paulie's fingers will be frantic in his hair. *Where's O'Meara this morning?* they'll say to him. *Has he found himself a gerbil?* The other fishgutters will be cursing over slabs of fillets. Their plastic gloves will be covered in blood. Strings of fishgut will have fallen on their boots. *That bastard's always late anyway.*

I should pull on my old jeans and whistle for a taxi, or hop on the trolley, or ride the bicycle through the hills, down to the warehouse, but the light this morning is curiously heavy, indolent, slow, and I feel like staying.

Enrique is coughing in the bedroom behind me, spitting into the pillow. It sounds like the rasp of the seals along the coastline cliffs farther up the California shore. His skin is sallow and tight around his jaw. The way he thrashes around in the bed reminds me of a baby corncrake I once took home after an oil slick in my hometown near Bantry Bay, continually battering its blackened wings against the cage to get out.

He should wake soon, and perhaps today he'll feel well enough to sit up, read a novel or a magazine. I bend down and pick up the large pieces of shattered glass from the floor. There's a long scar on the wall where I threw the jamjar. *That was smart, O'Meara, wasn't it?* I find two quarters and a few dimes scattered among the glass. There's an Irish five-penny piece on the floor too, an anachronism, a memory.

I flick a tiny shard of glass off my finger, and Enrique tosses again in bed. He is continually thinning, like the eggshell of a falcon, and soon the sheets will hardly ripple. I move to the bathroom and take a quick piss in the sink. Enrique has always said that it's a much better height and there's no risk of splashing the seat. Not too hygienic, but curiously pleasurable. My eyes are bloodshot in the mirror, and I notice the jowly look in my face. When I wash I can still smell yesterday's fish on my hands. We are down to the last bar of soap, and the water that comes through the tap has a red iron color to it. Back in the bedroom I pull on my jeans, a heavy-checked lumber shirt, and my black-peaked hat. I search in the pockets of my jeans and find three more dollars, then check my watch. Another hour late won't really matter. My coat hangs on the bedpost. I lean over him again and tell him that I will be back in a few moments. He doesn't stir. *Ah, isn't that just lovely, O'Meara? Out ya go and get breakfast for Enrique.*

The wind at my back hurries me along, down the street, past a row of saplings, over a child's hopscotch chalkmarks, to the deli, where Betty is working the counter. It's an old neighborhood store, the black-and-white floor tiles curled up around the edges. Betty is a large, dark-haired woman—capable, Enrique jokes, of owning her own zip code. She often wears tank tops, and the large flaps of flab that hang down from her underarms would be obscene on anybody else, but they seem to suit her. There's a barker on the other side of town, near City Lights Bookstore, who shouts about "Sweaty Betty" 's shows, but I've never had the guts to go in and see if it's her up there, jiggling onstage in the neon lights. Betty negotiates the aisles of the deli crabways, her rear end sometimes knocking over the display stands of potato chips. When she slices the ham the slabs are as thick as her fingers. There is a bell on the inside of the door, and when I come in she looks up from the cash register, closing the newspaper at the same time.

"The Wild Colonial Boy," she says. "What's the rush?"

"Late for work. Just gonna grab a few things."

"Still working down at the abattoir?"

"The warehouse. Gutting fish."

"Same difference." Her laugh resounds around the shop.

29

The tassels on the bosom of her white blouse bounce. Her teeth are tremendously white, but I notice her fingernails chewed down to the quick. The bell clangs and a couple of elderly Asians come in, followed by a man whom I recognize as a bartender down on Geary Street. Betty greets each of them with a fluttering wave.

I move up and down the aisles, looking at prices, fingering the $3.80 in my pocket. Coffee is out of the question, as are the croissants in the bakery case, which are a dollar apiece. An apple tart might do the trick however. Walking down the rows of food, other breakfasts come back to me—sausages and rashers fried in a suburban Irish kitchen with an exhaust fan sucking up the smoke, plastic glasses full of orange juice, cornflakes floating on milk, pieces of pudding in circles on chipped white plates, fried tomatoes and toast slobbered with butter. In the background Gay Byrne would talk on on the radio, while my late mother draped herself over the stove, watching the steam rise from the kettle. Mornings spinning off on my Raleigh to lectures at University, a bar of Weetabix in my jacket pocket. Once, champagne and strawberries in Sausalito with a lover who clawed his brown moustache between his teeth.

I reach for a small plastic jar of orange juice and a half dozen eggs in the deli fridge, two oranges and a banana from the fruit stand, then tuck a loaf of French bread under my arm. There is butter and jam at home, perhaps some leftover teabags. Betty sells loose cigarettes at twenty-five cents each. Two each for Enrique and me will do nicely. Tomorrow night, when I get my wages from the warehouse—Paulie will be there with his head bent over the checks morosely and some stray old fishermen will be coughing in from their boats—I will buy steak and vegetables. Not too much, though. Enrique has been having a hard time keeping his food down, and the blue bucket sits at the side of our bed, an ugly ornament.

I cart the groceries up to the cash register, and Betty cocks an eye at me.

"How's the patient?" she asks. "Haven't seen hide nor hair of him in the last three weeks."

"Still holed up in bed."

"Any news?"

"None, I'm afraid."

She shakes her head and purses her lips. I reach into my pocket for the change. "Can I get four of your smokes please?"

Betty reaches up above her for a box of Marlboro Lights and slides them on the counter, toward me. "My treat," she says. "Don't smoke 'em all at once, hon." I thank her and tuck them quickly in my shirt pocket. Betty leans over the counter and touches my left hand: "And tell that man of yours I want to see his cute little Argentinian ass in here."

"He'll be up and at it in a few days," I say, putting the groceries in a white plastic bag and hooking it over my wrist. "Thanks again for the smokes."

The door clangs behind me, and the street seems to open up in a wide sweep. Twenty cigarettes can make a man's day. I skip through the chalk marks—it's been years since I've hopscotched—and sit down on the curb, between a green Saab and an orange pickup truck, to light up. Looking down the street I can make out our balcony, above the tops of the cars, but there's no sign of Enrique.

Last night he almost cried when the cocaine coagulated in his sweat, but I scooped some off his belly and onto the mirror. He pushed it away and turned his face to the wall, looked up at a photograph of himself rafting the Parana River. The photo is fading now, yellowing around the edges. The way he leans forward in the boat, going down through a rapid, with his paddle about to strike the water, looks ineffably sad to me these days. He hasn't been near a river in years and hasn't gone outside for almost a month.

In the apartment we have unrolled our sleeping bags and use them as blankets over the bedsheets. Our television set is in the front window of the pawnshop, next to a hunting bow. The trust fund is dry, but Enrique is adamant that I don't call his father. The insurance people are gentle but unyielding. Sometimes I imagine a man at the very tip of Tierra del Fuego reaching his arms out toward the condors that flap their wings against the red air. He wonders where his son has gone.

Enrique sometimes talks of moving to the Pampas. His mind takes him there, and we are building a wooden fence together behind a ranch house. The grasses sweep along with a northward wind. At night we watch the sun swing downward behind a distant windmill.

Late at night he often wakes and babbles about his father's

cattle farm. When he was young he would go to the river with his friends. They would have swimming contests, holding against the rapids. Whoever stayed longest in one spot was the winner. In the late afternoons, he'd still be there, swimming stationary in the current, flailing away, without noticing that his friends were already halfway down the river. After the competition, they would stand in the water and catch fish with their hands. Then they'd light a campfire and cook the fish. It was Enrique who taught me how to gut when I first got the job down in the warehouse. With one smooth sweep of the finger you can take out all the innards.

When scrambling eggs I always make sure to add a little milk and whisk the fork around the bowl quickly so that none of the small stringy pieces of white will be left when they're cooked. The only disturbing thing about my mother's breakfasts were the long thin raw white pieces. The kitchen is small, with only room for one person to move. I lay the baguette on the counter and slice it, then daub butter on the inside. The oven takes a long time to warm up. In the meantime I boil water and put some teabags in the sunflower-patterned mugs.

I hear Enrique stir out of bed and move slowly toward the window. At first the noise startles me, but I'm glad he's awake. I hope he doesn't cut his feet on the stray glass—the doctor told us that the longer this goes on the harder it will be to stop a cut from bleeding.

Steam has gathered on the glass face of the oven clock. *You're late again, O'Meara, were ya picking petals offa roses?* I peel the oranges and arrange them in segments on the plate. *Or maybe you were spanking the monkey, is that it, O'Meara?* I hear the radio click on and a chair being dragged out onto the balcony. I hope he's put his scarf on under his dressing gown or else the chill will get to him.

I wish I could have seen him when I was down on the street, watched him sitting there, looking out over the white city, his hair dark and strewn like seaweed, the tufts on his chest curling toward his neck, his face chiselled, the scar on his chin worn like the wrongly tied knot of a Persian rug.

The eggs puff up and harden, sticking to the side of the saucepan. I scrape them off with a fork and then arrange the dollops on two plates. I've burnt the bread a little and the water is still not boiled. Amazing thing that, water. The molecules bouncing off each other at a huge rate of speed, passing on energy to one another, giving heat, losing heat. In the warehouse I spend my time thinking about these brutally stupid things, whittling the hours away. *There're lots of people in this town'd be happy to gut fish, bum-boy.* I put the bread on a third plate and wait. When the water finally boils I pour it on the teabags, making sure the little paper tabs stay outside the mugs. I hold the three plates in the shape of a shamrock in my right hand—I was a waiter before I met Enrique—and I grab the handles of both cups with my left forefinger and thumb.

The door to the bedroom is slightly ajar and I push it with

my left foot. It opens with a creak but Enrique doesn't turn in his chair on the balcony. Perhaps the traffic is too loud. I see him cough and then spit into one of our flowerpots. He leans back in the chair again. It's a little more gray outside now, the sun blocked by clouds. I see that he has picked up the last pieces of the jamjar and put them on the bedside table. The pillow has been turned over and there are no visible blood spots, but there is a cluster of stray black hairs on the bedsheets. Twenty-seven is too young to be going bald.

I move soundlessly across the room. His head is laid back in the chair now. The curtains on the French windows swish against my leg and the rings tinkle against the rod. I sidle up behind the chair, lean over him, hand him the tea, and he smiles. His face seems weathered, the eyes run into crowfeet, the brow heavy. We kiss and then he blows on the tea, the steam rising up. *Why the hell d'you wear those goddamn bracelets anyway, O'Meara?*

"I thought you were gone already," he says.

"In a few minutes. I thought it'd be nice to have breakfast."

"Wonderful." He reaches out for the plate. "I'm not sure if I can."

"It's all right. Eat as much as you like." I put my own plate down on the balcony floor and close the top button on my shirt to keep out the wind. Cars trundle along the street below. Some kids have taken over the hopscotch court. There is a tremendous freshness to the breeze coming up from the sea and it rifles through the trees. Enrique purses his lips, as if to speak, then lets them fall apart, and he looks along the street again, a small smile crackling the edges of his mouth. The bags under his eyes darken.

"I have some smokes too," I say. "Betty gave them to me. And some orange juice if you want it."

"Great." Enrique stabs gingerly at the eggs with his fork and moves the pieces of orange around. Then he reaches for a piece of bread and slowly tears the crust off. "Lovely day, isn't it?" he says, all of a sudden sweeping his arm out to the street.

"Gorgeous."

"Radio said that the high would be in the sixties."

"Grand weather for sitting around," I say.

"Lows tonight in the high forties."

"We'll sleep well."

He nods his head and shifts his body gently in the chair. A small piece of crust falls down into the lap of his dressing gown. He reaches for it and lays it on the side of the plate. "Nice eggs," he says.

"Wish I didn't have to go to the warehouse."

"We could just sit here and talk."

"We could," I say.

I watch him as he eddies the fork around the plate, but his eyes are drooping already. The cup of tea sits on the floor, by the edge of his chair. He leans his head back against the chair and sighs. His chest thumps like that of a small bird. The beginnings of sweat gather on his brow. I watch as the fork slides across the plate and nestles itself against the clump of food. I look down at the traffic passing beneath us, and all of a sudden I understand that we are in the stream, Enrique and I, that the traffic below us is flowing quite steadily, trying to carry us along, while all the time he is beating his arms against the current, holding still, staying in one place.

He sleeps and the breakfast grows cold.

In a few moments I will go to work and gut everything they bring me, but for now I watch this body of Enrique's, this house of sweat, this weedlot of proteins, slowly being assaulted.

Enrique once told me a story about starfish.

There was an oyster fisherman down the coast from Buenos Aires who farmed his own little area of the bay. He hadn't listened to the generations of fishermen who had gone before him, their advice, their tricks, their superstitions. All he knew was that starfish preyed on oysters. When they were dragged up in his nets he would take them and rip their symmetrical bodies in two neat pieces. He would fling them over the side of the boat and continue fishing. I imagine he was probably a bearded man with a rawboned laugh. But what he didn't know is that the starfish don't die when ripped, they regenerate themselves. For every one he tore, a second one came about. He wondered why there were so many starfish and so few oysters left, until he was told by an older fisherman. From then on, the fisherman left the starfish alone, although he could perhaps have taken

37

them to shore and dumped them behind some big gray rock or in a large silver dustbin on the pier where the children, on the way home from school, would fling them like stones.

There are times these days, strange times spent among these idle thoughts of mine, when I wonder why my fishermen don't come to me in the warehouse, amazed, cigarettes dangling from their lips, two fully grown starfish in their hands, saying, *Look at this O'Meara, look, for Christ's sake, can you imagine this?*

A BASKET FULL OF

WALLPAPER

S ome people said that he'd been a chicken-sexer during
  the forties, a pale and narrow man who had spent his days
interned in a camp for the Japanese near the mountains of
Idaho. Endless months spent determining whether chickens
were male or female. He had come to Ireland to forget it all. At
other times, the older men, elbows on the bar counter, invented heinous crimes for him. In Japan, they said, he had
attached electrical cords to the testicles of airmen, ritually sliced
prisoners with swords, operated slow drip torture on young
Marines. They said he had that sort of face. Dark eyes falling
down into sunken cheeks, a full mouth without any color, a
tiny scar over his right eye. Even the women created a fantastic
history for him. He was the fourth son of an emperor, or a
poet, or a general, carrying the baggage of unrequited love. To
us boys at school he was a kamikaze pilot who had gotten cold

feet, barrelling out in a parachute and somehow drifting to our town, carried by some ferocious, magical wave.

Osobe walked on the beach with his head slung low to the ground, stooping to collect stones. We would sometimes hide in the dunes, parting the long grass to watch him filling his trouser pockets with stones. He had a long rambling stride, sometimes walking for hours along the coast, while the gulls hurled themselves up from the strand, and small fishing boats bobbed on the sea. When I was twelve years old I saw him leap along the beach while a porpoise surfaced and resurfaced in the water, fifty yards away. Once Paul Ryan wrapped a note around a brick and flung it through the window of his cottage, one of a row of fifteen small houses in the center of our village. *Nip go home* said the note. The following day we noticed that the window had been covered with wallpaper and Paul Ryan went home from school with blood caked under his nose because we could no longer see through Osobe's front window.

Osobe had come to Ireland before I was born, sometime in the fifties. He was a curious sight in any Irish town, his black hair sticking out like conifer needles, his eyes shaded by the brim of his brown hat. He had bought the cottage, a dilapidated two-room affair, from an out-of-town landlord who thought that Osobe might just stay for a month or two. But, according to my father, a huge lorry carrying reams and reams of wallpaper pulled up to the cottage during the first summer of his visit. Osobe and two hefty Dubliners lifted all the paper into the house, and later he hung a sign on his front window: WALL-

PAPER FOR SALE—ASK INSIDE. There were mutterings about how the paper had been stolen, how it had been imported from Japan at a ridiculous price, undercutting the Irish wholesalers. Nobody bought any for a month until my Aunt Moira, who was infamous for having gotten drunk with Brendan Behan in a Republican pub in Dublin, knocked on his door and ordered a floral pattern with a touch of pink for her living room.

Osobe rode his black bicycle along the river out to her house. Rolls of paper, cans of glue, knives, and brushes were piled into the basket. My aunt said he did a wonderful job, although people muttered about her outside mass on Sunday mornings. "He was as quiet then as he is now," she told me. "No more noise out of him than a dormouse, and we should leave it that way. He's a good man who never done anyone a whit of harm." She laughed at the rumors that hung around him.

By the time I was born he was a fixture around town, no stranger than the newspaper editor whose handkerchiefs drooped from his trouser pockets, the shopkeeper who kept the footballs that landed in her back garden, the soldier who had lost his right hand while fighting for Franco. People nodded to him on the streets and, in Gaffney's pub, he was left alone over his morning pint of Guinness. He had a brisk trade going with the wallpaper, and occasionally, when Kieran O'Malley, the local handyman, was sick, he was called out to unblock a toilet or fix a crooked door. There was talk that he was seeing a young girl from Galway, a madwoman who walked around with a third sleeve sewn on her dresses. But that had about as much truth as all the other rumors—or less, in fact, since he was never seen to leave town, not even on his bicycle.

He spoke English haltingly and in the shops he would whisper for a packet of cigarettes or a jar of jam. He never wore his brown hat on Sundays. Girls giggled when he passed them in the street holding a red Japanese sun umbrella above his head.

I was sixteen years old when he hung a sign on his front door, looking for help with a wallpaper job. It was a hot summer, the ground was bone dry, and there were no seasonal jobs in the fields. My father moaned at the dinner table about the huge toll that emigration was having on his undertaking business. "Everyone's gone somewhere else to die," he'd say. "Even that Mrs. Hynes is hanging on for dear life." One evening my mother came and sat by my bed, mashing her fingers together nervously. She muttered under her breath that I should get some work with the Japanese man, that I was old enough now to put some bread on the table. I had noticed that in the bread that she baked at home, there were no currants anymore.

The following morning, in a blue wool sweater and old working trousers, I sidled down to his house and knocked on his door.

The cottage was filled with rolls of wallpaper. They were stacked on top of one another all around the living room, crowding in toward the small table and two wooden chairs. Most of the rolls were muted in color, but they made a strange collage, flowers and vines and odd shapes all meshed together.

The walls themselves had been papered with dozens of different types, and the smell of paste was heavy in the house. On the ground sat rows and rows of small paper dolls, the faces painted almost comically. An old philosopher, a young girl, a wizened woman, a soldier. A row of Japanese books stood against one wall. On top of them, a pan of sliced bread. Cigarette packages littered the floor. There was a collection of beach stones on the mantelpiece. I noticed lots of change and a few pound notes scattered around the cottage, and a twenty-pound note stuffed under a lamp. A kettle whistled on the stove and he filled up two china cups with tea.

"Welcome," he said. The saucer rattled in my fingers. "There is big job in house. You will help me?"

I nodded and sipped at the tea, which tasted peculiarly bitter. His hands were long and spindly, dotted with liver spots. A gray shirt slouched on his thin shoulders.

"You will go home and get bicycle, in this afternoon we start. Very good?"

We rode out together to the old Gorman house, which had lain empty for three years. Osobe whistled as we pedaled, and people stared at us from their cars and houses. Five rolls of pale green wallpaper were balanced in his front basket, and I carried two cans of paste in my right hand, steering the bicycle with the other. I saw Paul Ryan hanging out by the school, smoking a long cigar. "Ya get slanty eyes from wanking too much, Donnelly," he shouted, and I tucked my head down toward the handlebars.

The Gorman house had been bought by an American mil-

lionaire just three months before. There were schoolboy rumors that the American drove a huge Cadillac and had five
blond daughters who would be fond of the local disco and, on
excellent authority, were known to romp behind haystacks. But
there was nobody there when we arrived on our bicycles.
Osobe produced a set of keys from his overalls and walked
slowly through the house, pointing at the walls, motes of dust
kicking up from behind him. We made five trips on the bikes
that day, carrying rolls of wallpaper and paste each time. At the
end of the day, after I had brought a ladder over my shoulder
from his house, he produced a brand new ten-pound note and
offered it to me.

"Tomorrow we start," he said, and then he bowed slightly.
"You are fast on bicycle," he said.

I went outside. The sun was settling over the town. I heard
Osobe humming in the background as I leaped on my bike and
rode toward home, the money stuffed down deep in my pocket.

That summer I read books in my bedroom and I wanted Osobe
to tell me a fabulous story about his past. I suppose I wanted to
own a piece of him, to make his history belong to me.

It would have something to do with Hiroshima, I had decided, with the children of the pikadon, the flash boom. There
would be charred telegraph poles and tree trunks, a wasteland
of concrete, a single remaining shell of a building. People with
melted faces would run wildly through the streets. Bloated

corpses would float down the Ota River. The slates on the
roofs of houses would bubble. He would spit on the American
and British soldiers as they sat under burnt cherry blossom
trees, working the chewing gum over in their mouths. Perhaps,
in his story, he would reach out for the festered face of a young
girl. Or massage the burnt scalp of a boy. A woman friend of
his would see her reflection in a bowl of soup and howl. Maybe
he would run off toward the hills and never stop. Or perhaps he
would simply just walk away down narrow roads, wearing
wooden sandals, a begging bowl in his hands. It would be a
peculiar Buddhist hell, that story of his, and a B-29 would
drone in constantly from the clouds.

But Osobe stayed silent almost the whole time as he stood in
that big old house and spread paste on the walls in long smooth
motions, humming gently as the house began to take on color.
"Sean," he would say to me in his comically broken English,
with his face cocked into a smile, "someday you will be great
wallpaper man. You must think how important this job. We
make people happy or sad if we do bad job."

He would buy big bottles of Club Orange and packets of
Goldgrain biscuits and spread them out on the ground during
lunchtime. He brought a radio one morning and his old body
swayed with movement as he tuned in to a pop station from
Dublin. Once, for a joke, he swiped a ladder away from me and
left me hanging from a door ledge. He was deft with a knife,
slicing the wallpaper in one smooth motion. At the end of the
day he would smoke two cigarettes, allowing me a puff at the
end of each one. Then he would sit, lotus-legged, in front of a

newly decorated wall and nod, smiling gently, rocking back and forth.

"What is Japan like?" I asked him one evening as we were cycling home, my palms sweaty.

"Like everywhere else. Not as beautiful like this," he said, sweeping his arms around the fields and hills.

"Why did you come here?"

"So long ago." He pointed at his nose. "Don't remember. Sorry."

"Were you in the war?"

"You ask lots of questions."

"Somebody told me you were in Hiroshima."

He laughed uproariously, slapping his thighs. "I have no answer." He rode silently for a while. "Hiroshima was sad place. Japanese don't talk about."

"Were you in Hiroshima?" I asked again.

"No, no," he said. "No, no."

"Do you hate Americans?"

"Why?"

"Because . . ."

"You are very young. You shouldn't think these things. You should think of making good job with wallpaper. That is important."

We rode out to the house at eight every morning. The lawn was dry and cracked. The third floor windows were black with soot. When the radio played it could be heard all over the house. Osobe worked with tremendous energy. In the hot afternoons he rolled up his sleeves and I could see his sinewy arms. Once, when the radio told us of an earthquake in Japan, he blanched and said that the country was suffering from too much pain.

In the evenings I started going down to the bridge with my friends to drink flagons of cider with the money I held back from my parents. I began to buy my own cigarettes. I read books about World War II and created fabulous lies about how he had been in that southern Japanese city when the bomb had been dropped, how his family had been left as shadows on the town hall walls, dark patches of people on broken concrete. He had been ten miles from the epicenter of the blast, I said, in the shade of a building, wearing billowy orange carpenter pants and a large straw hat. He was flung to the ground, and when he awoke, the city was howling all around him. He had reeled away from the horror of it all, traveling the world, ending up in the west of Ireland. My friends whistled through their teeth. Under the bridge they pushed the bottle toward me.

Occasionally my mother and father asked me about Osobe, muted questions, probings, which they slid in at dinnertime after I had handed over most of my wages.

"He's a strange one, that one," said my father.

"Hiding something, I'd guess," my mother would respond, the fork clanging against her teeth.

"Bit of a mad fellow, isn't he, Sean?"

"Ah, he's not too bad," I said.

"People say he lived in Brazil for a while."

"God knows, he could have," said my mother.

"He doesn't tell me anything," I said.

For all I really knew, he had just wandered to our town for no good or sufficient reason and decided to stay. I had an uncle in Ghana, an older brother in Nebraska, a distant cousin who worked as a well digger near Melbourne, none of which struck me as peculiar. Osobe was probably just one of their breed, a wanderer, a misfit, although I didn't want him to be. I wanted him to be more than that.

We worked through that hot summer together, finished the Gorman house and started on a few others. I grew to enjoy clambering along the roads on our bicycles in the morning, slapping paste on the walls, inventing tales about him for my friends down under the bridge. Some of my friends were working in the chipper, others were bringing in the tired hay, and a couple were selling golf balls down at the club. Every evening I continued with Osobe stories for them, their faces lit up by the small fire we kept going. We all slurped at the bottles, fascinated by the terror and brilliance of it all. Fireballs had raged throughout the city as he fled, I told them. People ran with sacks of rice in their melted hands. A Shinto monk said prayers over the dead. Strange weeds grew in clumps where the plum trees once flowered, and Osobe left the city, half-naked, his throat and eyes burning.

Osobe opened the door to me one morning toward the end of summer. "All the jobs almost done," he said. "We celebrate with cup of tea."

He guided me gently by the arm to the chair in the middle
of the room. Looking around I noticed that he had been
wallpapering again. He had papered over the old pattern. There
were no bubbles, no stray ends, no spilled paste around the
edges. I imagined him staying up late at night, humming as he
watched the colors close in on him. The rest of the cottage was
a riot of odds and ends—dishes and teacups, an Oriental fan,
wrapped slices of cheese, a futon mattress rolled in the corner.
There was a twenty-pound note sitting on the small gas heater
near the table. Another ten-pound note lay on the floor, near
the table. His brown hat was hung up on the door. There were
paintbrushes everywhere.

"You did good job," he said. "Will you go soon school?"

"In a few weeks."

"Will you one day paper? Again. If I find you job?" he said.

Before I could answer he had sprung to his heels to open the
front door for a marmalade-colored cat, which had been
scratching at the door. It was a stray. We often saw it slinking
around the back of the chipper, waiting for some scraps. John
Brogan once tried to catch it with a giant net but couldn't. It
scurried away from everyone. Osobe leaned down on his hunkers and, swooping his arms as if he were going to maul it, he
got the cat to come closer. It was almost a windmill motion,
smoothly through the air, his thin arms making arcs. The cat
stared. Then, with a violent quickness, Osobe scooped it up,
turned it on its back, pinned it down with one hand and
roughly stroked his other hand along its belly. The cat leaned its
head back and purred. Osobe laughed.

For a moment I felt a vicious hatred for him and his quiet ways, his mundane stroll through the summer, his ordinariness, the banality of everything he had become. He should have been a hero or a seer. He should have told me some incredible story that I could carry with me forever. After all, he had been the one who had run along the beach parallel to a porpoise, who filled his pockets full of pebbles, who could lift the stray orange cat in his fingers.

I looked around the room for a moment while he hunched down with the cat, his back to me. I was hoping to find something, a diary, a picture, a drawing, a badge, anything that would tell me a little more about him. Looking over my shoulder I reached across to the gas heater, picked up the twenty-pound note and stuffed it in my sock, then pulled my trousers down over it. I sat at the wooden table, my hands shaking. After a while Osobe turned and came over toward me with the cat in his arms, stroking it with the same harsh motion as before. With his right hand he reached into his overalls and gave me a hundred pounds in ten new notes. "For you school." I could feel the other twenty-pound note riding up in my sock, and as I backed out the door a sick feeling rose in my stomach.

"You did very good job," he said. "Come back for visit."

It was only afterward that I realized I never got the cup of tea he offered.

That night, full of cider, I stumbled away from the bridge and walked down along the row of houses where Osobe lived. I climbed around the back of the house, through the hedge, along by some flowerpots, rattling an old wheelbarrow as I moved up to the window. He was there, slapping paste on the wall in gentle arcs. I counted five separate sheets, and the wall must have come a good quarter of an inch closer to him. I wanted him to be sloppy this time, not to smooth the sheets out, to wield the knife in a slipshod way, but he did the job as always, precise and fluid. The whole time he was humming and I stood, drunk, rattling the change from the twenty-pound note in my pocket.

Years later, when I was acquiring an English accent in the East End of London, I got a letter from my father. Business was still slow and a new wave of emigration had left its famous scars. Old Mrs. Hynes still hadn't kicked the bucket. Five of the council houses were empty now, and even the Gorman house had been sold once more. The American in his Cadillac had never arrived with his five blond daughters. The hurling team had lost all its matches again this year. There was a bumper crop of hay.

On the last page of the letter he told me that Osobe had died. The body was not discovered for three days, until my Aunt Moira called around with a basket of fruit for him. My father said that when he went into the house, the stench was so bad that he almost vomited. Children gathered at the front door with their hands held to their noses. But there was a whiparound made in Gaffney's pub that extended out to the streets. People threw generous amounts of money in a big brown hat that the owner of the chipper carried from door to door. My aunt chose him a fine coffin, although someone said that he might have been offended by it, that he should have been sent back to Japan to be cremated. She scoffed at the suggestion and made a bouquet of flowers for him.

There was a party held the night of the funeral, and rumors were flung around according to the depths of the whiskey bottle—but more or less everyone was sure now that he had been a victim of Hiroshima. All the young boys who had worked for him in the summer months had heard vivid details of that frightening August morning. He had run from the city in a pair of wooden sandals. All his family had been killed. They had been vaporized. He was a man in flight. By the early, sober hours of the morning, my father added, the talk was that Osobe was a decent sort, no matter what his history was. Over the years he had employed many young men to work with him, treated them fairly, paid them handsomely, and confided in them about his life. They laughed at how strange his accent had become at the end of it all—when he went to the shop to buy cigarettes he would lean over the counter and whisper for *pack of fags, prease*. The sight of him carrying that big ladder on his bicycle would be sorely missed around town.

But the strangest thing of all, my father said, was that when he had gone into the house to recover the body, the room had seemed very small to him. It was customary to burn the bedsheets and scrape the paper from the walls when someone had been dead that long. But he took a knife to the paper and discovered it was a couple of feet thick, though it didn't seem so at first glance. Layers and layers of wallpaper. It looked as if Osobe had been gathering the walls into himself, probably some sort of psychological effect brought on by the bomb. Because the wallpaper had been so dense, the town council had decided simply to knock down the house, burying everything Osobe owned in the rubble. There had been no clues there, no letters, no medical papers, nothing to indicate that he had come from that most horrific of moments.

I rode my bicycle around London that night. I plowed along to no particular place, furious in the pedals, blood thumping, sweat pouring from my brow. The chain squeaked. A road in Ireland rose up in front of me—a road of grass grown ochre in the summer heat, a thin figure in a brown hat along the river, a cat the color of the going sun, a wall brought closer in slow movements, a road that wound forever through dry fields toward a gray beach, a road long gone. I found myself down by the Thames in the early morning. I dropped a single twenty-pound note into the water and watched it as it spun away, very slowly, very simply, with the current, down toward some final sea to fete the dead, their death, and their dying too.

THROUGH THE FIELD

See, the thing about it is that klein grass was about going out to head. It was hot out there—like Kevin says, it was hotter than a three-peckered goat—and I was keen on getting the whole job done as soon as possible, before we got ourselves a rain and lost all the nutrient to seed. I never seen a field look so good, a big sweep of grass almost four foot tall, running down to the creekbed where Natalie found that rattler one time. When the sun fell on it right and the wind blew from up along the creek, the field looked like someone had given it a real good haircut.

I wished I owned it, but we were renting it from Cunningham. It was going to take about three days, what with all the cutting, crimping, and swathing. We'd have ourselves about forty, fifty round bales and we were going to make a nice little profit, I could tell. Kevin figured on maybe buying some wallpaper for Natalie's bedroom—she's gone outgrown that pink kind—or maybe just him and Delicia having a little easier living, put their feet up some for a day or two. I was wanting to get a valve job done on my pickup.

We were only able to work the field at the weekend, Kevin and me, seeing as how we were at the State School during the week. That Friday evening Kevin was hollering to fill the tractor with gas so we could get a start. He's a hard worker, Kevin is, with big ropy arms. He's always itching to get going. You watch him, even at lunchtime, and his foot's tapping. I was ready too. I had my new boots that Ellie bought me at Reid's. We wanted to cut as much as we could, up until it got dark. We were filling the tractor right enough, but then we started getting into all that stuff about Stephen Youngblood, the kid that murdered that guy over near Nacogdoches. Kevin, he got the chills when I told him what that boy had said. He started shivering, Kevin did, and he went on home to gather up mine and his family. That night we hardly got nothing done.

I been doing the grounds maintenance at the State School for the best part of three years now, and in all that time I never seen a man want to know something so bad. Ferlinghetti, he come down from the University of Texas, like they sometimes do, for his work study. He got assigned the juvenile capital offenders. He wasn't young like the rest of the students. He was about my age. He was kind of fat, and once I heard one of the boys say that he was nothing but ten pounds of shit wrapped in a five pound bag. Which made me laugh. But he wasn't *that* fat, and he had these blue eyes, blue as the blue you get on a winter's morning. And, boy, could he get those kids to talk.

Truth be told, most of the staff at the State School don't like the social work students much. They come in on their work placement, thinking they can save the world. There's nobody can save the world except maybe Jesus, but even Jesus must have had an off day when He made most of the kids at the State School. And maybe when He made the place itself, because it don't much look like a prison. It's like a complex with a fence around it and cottages where the kids live. But it's big and open, with grass and trees and flowers, which I guess is good because it gives me and Kevin a job. There ain't no uniforms on the kids neither. The thing that shocks people the most is that the place doesn't shock them. It just looks ordinary. The kids out there, walking in double-file groups along the sidewalk, with the security guards going around in vans and station wagons. And no guns, not a one.

Most of those kids—even the ones in there for murder—look like the sort you see hanging out down by Sonic or skateboarding outside the 7-Eleven. I thought Stephen Youngblood was just another one that got caught up in a mess and couldn't get out. But Ferlinghetti, he thought he was onto something big for him and his head-shrinking business.

Stephen was small and blond and wiry with acne all over. You could drown him just by spitting on him. He had eyeglasses, but kept them hid in his back pocket. Embarrassed, I guess. He always walked with his head down, like he's hiding something. You wouldn't believe that he'd done what he done. Most days him and Ferlinghetti would be outside, on the bench under the oak tree. Ferlinghetti'd be talking to him, staring right into his face, hands on his belly, nodding his head up and down. He looked like a buzzard on a branch, searching for some dead meat.

The kids were supposed to get about twenty-five minutes of counseling a week, but Ferlinghetti, damnit, he must have talked Stephen's ear off for a couple of hours each time.

I was out there the first time they talked, working on a flower bed near the bench, and Stephen was giving him the normal kind of stuff the kids give new counselors. "I took the life of William Harris on December ninth two years ago. I got a thirty-year determinate sentence." They learn to say it that way in the Capital Offenders Group. After a while they just say it, not a hint of emotion, because they said it hundreds of times.

Stephen was flicking his blond hair away from his eyes, gazing straight ahead, when Ferlinghetti just, boom, changed the subject. Now, most of them counselors they get all serious and sad-like, then say: "Would you like to talk about it, Stephen?" And Stephen'd say, "Yeah, s'pose so," just because he knows he'd be up the creek without a goddamn paddle if he says no. Then the counselor would say: "Well, Stephen, how do you *feel* about it?" And Stephen, he'd say: "Bad." And on and on, until the counselor goes off to write up his CF 114.

But not Ferlinghetti. He just looks at Stephen and nods. Then he starts talking about baseball, football, and heavy metal.

I damn near shit myself laughing, kneeling down there with the trowel in my hand. I stayed down there in the flower bed and listened as they talked about some drummer from England who got his arm chopped off in a car accident. Then Ferlinghetti said bye, walking off, his big ass waddling like a duck. And Stephen, he looked like he'd been slapped with a stick.

After that they started meeting all the time. And always on the concrete bench under the oak tree. Most of the other counselors, they like to get one of the offices or something for privacy, but not Ferlinghetti. Out in the open, that was him. And, man, did he get that boy to talk up a storm.

Me and Stephen, we worked together sometimes too. The kids get to do some of the flowers and the weed-eating, depending on their level. Stephen was doing pretty good—he was a senior—and he got to work with me. There's about three hundred kids, maybe twenty capital offenders, and you hear it all. There's some in there did nothing more than piss on their momma's toothbrush. But there's one who hung babies up by Christmas ribbons when a drug deal went wrong. Another who just blew his friend away for a vial of crack. One girl knifed her old man forty times.

Kevin, he's different from me. He's been working there twelve years, and he doesn't like to hear the stories no more. He says after a while you don't want to hear anything. You walk around with your head down and you mow the lawn with the noisiest goddamn lawnmower you can find, so that your ears get to ringing and you can't even hear the bell sounding for lunch. Even when Delicia comes along to pick him up at the front gate every day, he gets in the front of the station wagon, she asks him what's going on, and he just says, same ol', same ol', darling.

Me and Kevin planted the field in spring. Cunningham lent us the tractor and the other equipment, we plowed the field in late March, then sowed the klein grass the next day. That night, when we finished the sowing, we took ourselves a bottle and sat down at the edge of the creek and had ourselves a good time.

We took care of that field, Kevin and me, even though we didn't own it. Lord knows why we wanted to do it. One night we was just sitting around, shooting the shit, and both of us got to talking about ranching. See, last year there was a drought and some of the ranchers were low on hay for the cattle. We just wanted to start off with something small. Next year we're going to plant ourselves a proper crop. But Kevin has a friend works in the feed store on Polk Street who said he could get us some free grass seed, and we said okay. The field was five miles down the road and it was lying idle. We called old man Cunningham and he laughed at first. Said he didn't have time for fooling around. But we got it, in the end, pretty darn cheap too.

At night we'd come home from the State School and get a few beers and sit down and watch the thing grow. Klein grass has a broad leaf and a narrow stem. It gets up to near four foot.

It was mighty nice out there. We'd sit on the back of my pickup and watch the stars. Sometimes, when the sky was clear, Kevin would point out the satellites moving on through the stars. Every now and then you'd hear a coyote howl. I wanted to shoot those critters—used to be you could get some money for killing them—but Kevin said they never done anyone any harm. I suppose he's right. There's enough killing without having to start on the coyotes. When Kevin began in the State School twelve years ago there was hardly any kids who had done murder. Now they're all over the place. It gets you to wondering.

Kevin brings little Natalie out to the field a lot. She plays on the dirt road and sometimes climbs trees. But it scared the living daylights out of Kevin when Natalie found the rattlesnake down in the creekbed. She was six then and damn nearly got bit. I leave my Robert at home. He's just four years old and don't need to be messing around with snakes.

That Friday night we were supposed to start cutting the field. The following day we were going to cut some more, crimp it and lay it out in nice neat swaths. Then we were going to turn it so it dried evenly and, the next day, bale it. As it happened, we ended up being late with the whole deal, seeing how Kevin took the story about Stephen. At first he wasn't listening much, I was just babbling on. But then he looked at me, bug-eyed, like I'd told him the end of the world was coming.

Ferlinghetti got everything out of Stephen except why he gave himself up. I never seen anyone work a kid so hard for a tiny bit of information. I listened most days that I could, whenever they were out there on the bench. What I can't believe is how Stephen opened up to Ferlinghetti, telling him nearly every damn bit, but not the bit he really wanted to hear.

Once I seen Ferlinghetti hand him some Red Man, which is against the rules. It was raining pretty heavy but Ferlinghetti had himself an umbrella and they were huddled up close on the bench. I was walking over to one of the cottages and I seen him take the pack of Red Man out of his overcoat and give it to Stephen. But I do that too, sometimes. I have a can of Skoal and some kid's working with me, just dying for a dip, so you give him a pinch. It's only human. I suppose Ferlinghetti knew he could get Stephen to talk if he gave him some tobacco.

Stephen was fourteen when he did the killing, living in a trailer out near the Piney Woods. He'd been in one of them chicken-eating Baptist homes for a few years after some petty thievery, but his momma had taken him back. He'd watch a lot of TV and play with Nintendo. His momma was whoring around while his father was off out west, working the oilfields.

She was getting these pretty regular visits from this Bill Harris guy who was married and lived outside Nacogdoches. Nothing but cheap plyboard in the trailer and Stephen, he can hear all of it, the grunting and moaning and slapping and screaming. He gets mad and takes a baseball bat to Harris, who's laying in bed. He gets a couple of licks in, but Harris ups and kicks Stephen in the mouth, sending him to the hospital, where he has to get eight stitches.

Stephen gets himself out of the hospital and decides to take a visit over to Harris's wife to tell her what her husband's at. He gets on his ten-speed Huffy and rides over there. Except he gets tired halfway and decides to steal himself a truck, one of those Toyota pickups that just has YO on the back tailgate. He speeds on over there. This woman, Mrs. Harris, or whatever her name is, takes Stephen into her trailer. She sits him down at the kitchen table.

Stephen tells Ferlinghetti that the weird thing is that this Mrs. Harris—she's a redhead—don't even flinch when she finds out her husband's screwing around. She rises up from the table, puts her arms around Stephen, then starts rubbing her fingers up and down his chest saying thank you, thank you, thank you for telling me. Opening the buttons and all. Working her way down to his zipper. He's fourteen. Walks around all day long with a boner anyway, let alone when some old lady is doing him.

He's telling Ferlinghetti all this. That's what's killing me. He's telling Ferlinghetti about how he's getting done, how she's leaving lipstick on Russell the Love Muscle, how she looks like Woody Woodpecker down there with the red hair. Ferlinghetti lets him say things like that. Both of them look very serious, out there on the bench.

Anyway, that night Stephen goes home. Dumps the YO truck out on the edge of town. When he gets back Harris is gone.

His momma has made him some chicken-fried steak. She never cooks normally, always eating those Sonic burgers. He sits himself down at the table and eats real slow. She asks if his mouth is hurting him, and he tells her it's all right. He sees one of Harris's bandannas outside the bedroom door, but he just walks on by it.

He gets to visiting Mrs. Harris a couple of times a week, going out there on his Huffy. Harris, he's out in the oilfields, he don't know a goddamn thing about what his wife's doing. The redhead, she's telling Stephen how cute he is and all. Making him sandwiches and iced tea. Sitting on the concrete blocks, waving to him when he leaves. Stephen, he's in hog heaven.

Anyway, Harris comes home early to his trailer one week. Nobody expecting him. Stephen is there, lying in bed with the redhead, like a regular soap opera. Harris picks him up out of the bed and slaps him around. Stephen gets beat up pretty bad again and leaves on his ten-speed. When he comes back two hours later he's got a hunting rifle, a Marlin, that he's stolen from the gun rack of a pickup. Parks the truck. Goes around the back. Stands up on the ball of the trailer, where he can look into the bedroom. Harris is there boning his wife. Stephen's done himself some hunting before and says he's an ace with the rifle on Nintendo. He shoots him straight in the forehead. Harris flops to the floor. Stephen opens the door of the trailer and tells Mrs. Harris that she should get packed, that they're leaving. He wants her to go to Florida. He's seen Florida on the TV.

Harris is still alive on the floor. Stephen wants Mrs. Harris to say, "I love you, Stephen," in front of her old man. He's flipped out, Stephen has. And she's going plumb crazy. She's bent over her husband, sobbing. Then Stephen shouts at her: "Kiss me!" He's fourteen years old. "Kiss me!" She gets up and kisses him on the lips. Then he goes over to Harris, puts the gun down the man's throat, pulls the trigger, and kills him. He shoots Harris twice more, in the chest. All the time Mrs. Harris is just standing there, screaming.

Ferlinghetti, I guess he sees it as one of these mother complex things, because he's asking Stephen if he loves his mom and if he thought Mrs. Harris was his mom, that sort of thing. But, more than that, he's asking all the time what happened afterward and why Stephen gave himself up. They're sitting on the bench a couple of days a week, and he keeps coming at it all sorts of different ways. Eventually he just says it straight out.

"So, dude,"—that's what's cracking me up, this guy Ferlinghetti says "dude" and "dissing" and "cool" and "wild" and all—"why did you give yourself up to the cops?"

And Stephen, he don't say nothing. He just keeps on saying "because" over and over.

Stephen has already told him about how he ran into the forest after he shot and killed old man Harris. How the cops came and flooded the place. How he hid himself behind a tree and was just waiting for a chance to go back and ask the redhead if she wants to go to Florida. That's all he wants, to go down to the beaches with all the skinny women. How he wasn't scared of the cops, not a bit. He was sure they were going to get away. He was even going to leave a note for his mom. *Gone to Florida, see you soon.* The cops and the ambulance and the fire people are there all over the place.

At one point he gets so goddamn daring that he sneaks up to the back of the trailer and peeks in the window where the cops are taking photographs. Ferlinghetti don't believe that, I can tell, but Stephen doesn't care. He just says, what's the point in lying? I killed the man, everybody knows that.

So, he goes back into the forest. The sun is going down. He stays there a couple of hours, then just walks up to the police, who are all having coffee on the front steps of the trailer, and gives himself up.

Ferlinghetti asks again, says it's very important to him, starts giving this crap about how Stephen needs someone to respect him, that sort of thing, but Stephen still says "because." I'm just sitting there, in the flower bed, listening to all this. Once or twice Stephen turns around and looks at me. I just look down, pretending I'm not interested.

Later that afternoon we're out there digging and raking a flower bed, me and Stephen. There's some other workers there too, but they're feeling lazy, taking a load off their feet. I'm just digging away, and Stephen, he's sort of puttering with the rake. He's got those long skinny arms. For some reason he's wearing his eyeglasses, which he don't normally do. He's got some of that brown powder stuff on his face that the kids use to cover up their zits. He looks awful sad. It takes him a long old time to pull that rake along the ground even just a little bit.

Kevin's way over on the other side of the fence, near the staff houses, weed-eating. So I'm asking Stephen what he thinks of the Cowboys and the Oilers and all, except I get to thinking that I must sound like Ferlinghetti, asking all these questions, so I stop. I don't want to sound like no shrink. I'm just turning some soil, whistling away, thinking about how that night me and Kevin are due to start work on the field. I think maybe I'll go home and get myself a big old plate of steak, maybe some of that Gatorade that keeps you going. I'm looking at the sky and thinking it may stay clear, when Stephen turns to me. He looks straight at me.

"I was scared of the dark," he says.

First thing I'm thinking he's saying something about a darkie, which is weird since I think you only hear that word in old movies. But then I catch on. He's still looking at me, but I have no idea why he's telling me this. I ain't never asked him, but maybe he saw me listening to him and Ferlinghetti, so he figures I want to know. But he's just staring away into space. His mouth is quivering. His eyes are all red around the edges. This don't look like a boy who put a gun in a man's mouth and spilled his brains out on the floor, who stole them trucks, slept with that woman, all those things. He looks like an ordinary kid. He's just standing there, with the rake in his hands, looking out over the fence.

"I was out there in the forest and it got dark," he says. "I'd never been in the dark like that before."

I took to digging a little deeper in the soil and said nothing. I thought about Ferlinghetti and what he might get out of that. Stephen was scared of nothing else—not scared of killing a man, that's for sure, or stealing, or boning away whenever he got the chance. I knew it was weird. Guess he didn't have his TV or nothing out there. Guess that's what maybe he was scared of. I just nodded my head and said, I know what you mean, man, I know what you mean.

I'm telling Kevin all this and his face just drains. We're putting the gas in the tractor. He's holding the big red five-gallon can and I got the funnel. For some reason his hands start to shake like he's got the chills and some of that gas is spilling down the side of the tractor. "Scared of the dark," says Kevin, repeating it over and over. He puts the last drop of gas in the tank and then he tells me that he'll be back in a moment. I see him hightail off toward my pickup and slam the door. He leaves a trail of dust on the dirt road that runs through the center of our field. I get on the tractor to fire her up, but Kevin has the keys.

So I just sit myself down on the ground and poke a little stick in a mound of fire ants and watch the little bastards scuttle. Millions of them. Once I heard someone say that the ants can build a nest that goes fifteen feet down in the ground. They can also kill a human baby if there are enough of them. They start to crawl up my boots, so I climb up on the tractor and look out over the field.

I'm thinking that it sure is getting late. I can see some red sky in the west. There's even a star up there already. The last of the buzzards are in the sky. I wonder where it is they sleep at night. One thing for sure, those crickets don't sleep. They start chirping so it sounds like a song. It's almost fully night when I look up and there is Kevin coming down the road in the pickup truck. He has his whole family with him, the whole dadgum lot, his wife Delicia, his sons Lawrence and Myron, his girl Natalie. Then I see, sitting in the back of the truck, my Ellie and Robert. Everyone's quiet. Normally they're all shouting up a storm and laughing when they get together.

Kevin gets out of the truck with this strange look on his face. He's wearing his work shirt, and the sleeves are rolled way up on his arms. His face is full of wrinkles. His eyes all serious. He gets everyone to line up at the edge of the field behind him, in a row. Ellie's in her night gown and slippers. Her hair is in curlers. Delicia, she's carrying Myron in her arms because he's so small. Lawrence has himself a football tucked under his arm. I do a little shadow boxing with Robert, but he's quiet as a mouse. That klein grass is so big that it's over all the kids' heads. Nobody's saying anything. It's all quiet. Except for the crickets.

Kevin gets me to stand at the end of the line and then he starts walking through the field. Everyone just steps on along behind him, but pretty soon he gets to jogging and we all jog after him, brushing away the grass with our hands, until he goes faster and faster and we're hightailing it through that field, the grass parting in our way. I hear the kids laughing, then Delicia gives a chuckle, then Ellie hollers something crazy. I'm holding onto Robert's hand. He's kicking at the stalks as we go. Kevin is whooping. My own body gets kind of loose and I find myself damn near dancing through the field. I haven't danced like that since the club in Giddings burned down.

Well, it must have looked plumb stupid, us running through the field like that, with our kids, when we had so much work to do. But I was stumbling along, hearing everyone laughing, holding on to my little boy, when I looked up beyond the top of the grass and saw how dark the sky had gotten, how big and heavy it was, how much it had come right down on top of us. We were laughing, but I knew right there and then what Kevin was doing. He was no fool.

STOLEN CHILD

Padraic closes the heavy oak door of the children's home and steps out into the Brooklyn morning light. He looks across the river to where the sun is coming up like a stabwound, leaving smudges of dirty light on the New York City skyline. He pulls up the hood of his coat and steps across the road. In the background he hears one of the boys kicking at the wooden door, a dull rhythmic thud. A young girl screams from the third-floor window. In the distance a police siren flares. *Christ,* he thinks, *no day for a wedding.*

He pulls his dark blue anorak up around his shoulders, cups his hands, and lights the last of his cigarettes. He inhales the smoke to the bottom of his lungs, adjusts his glasses, and looks back at the home where he just clocked off the graveyard shift.

A clutch of blind children have their heads stuck out the bars of the lower windows. One of the girls, her hair a shock of orange, is thrashing her head against the bars. The whites of her eyes loll obscenely in her head. He shrugs his shoulders to indicate to her that it's not his fault, but, catching himself, he turns away, then pulls hard again on the cigarette. Padraic hears another shout from inside the home. He turns and watches a bread van cough along the street. The exhaust fumes languish in the air, and for a moment he thinks about letting the smoke carry him along, away down the dark puddled road, to some- where very different.

At ten o'clock last night, little Marcia, only fourteen years old, tried to slit her wrists with a tin mirror. She cut a narrow scar perpendicular to the veins while Tammy screamed over and over again that she was messing up, that the way to do it was to slice longways along the vein, rip it good and deep. When the lads in the boys' unit found out that one of the girls had tried to do herself in, a near-riot had broken out. Jimi set fire to the couch in the living room. Chocolate Charlie put his foot through the glass case of the stereo, and two other boys had to be restrained. Nearly all the kids, those forgotten blind children, the snot rags of society, had spent the night beating their brains against the walls repeatedly—like birds with broken wings, un- able to get off the ground.

Padraic flings the cigarette butt to the ground. He walks toward the subway station, sweeping the bits and pieces of litter out of his way with his feet. In one of the houses he hears a radio burst to life. A curtain opens and a woman's face fills a top windowpane. An old man in a mangy overcoat is out on the steps playing the Jewish harp and slurping on a bottle of Miller. He nods and offers the bottle, but Padraic gives a quick flick of the head sideways and the old man smiles.

"Too early for the sloppin'?" he asks.

"Too early for anything," says Padraic.

The steps down to the subway station smell, as usual, of stale urine, and Padraic skips down them three at a time, fishing in his pocket for a token. Nothing but loose change. He left all the tokens at home last night. He takes a quick look. Nobody in the booth and hardly anyone else around, except two young nurses shivering in the cold, a kid in a *Van Halen Kicks Ass* T-shirt, and a spindly little businessman reading a newspaper down at the end of the platform. He vaults the turnstile, hustles down to the platform, and waits for the wind to be sucked through the tunnel, carrying the clang of an engine.

When the D train finally comes, it's a local. He sits in a carriage alone, the seat bedecked with graffiti, and wonders if Orla, his wife, will be awake when he gets back to their flat. It'll be nice to curl up beside her and let the morning pass. Or wake her to get her to massage the knots in his neck.

In Brighton Beach he turns the key quietly in the apartment door and tiptoes into the bedroom where Orla is sleeping, a copy of Philip Larkin's *High Windows* on her chest. He picks up the book and skims through it quickly, leans over her, kisses her on the cheek.

"No day for a wedding," he says.

Padraic had come far across an incomprehensible ocean, from a place called Leitrim, and when Dana first heard him talk she thought he must have swallowed a very tiny insect or bird that made his voice the way it was. He stood in the middle of the common room while the other counselors introduced him, *Padraic Keegan is going to be our new social worker, now everybody say hello.* She ran up to him, scouring her fingers through his wiry hair, fingering the side of his acne-creviced face, lifting his glasses and trying to touch his eyes until a counselor barked at her to stop. Later, alone, she wondered whether it was a cricket or a thrush or a praying mantis that Padraic had swallowed.

She was sixteen, well into the awkward throes of adolescence, and she wore dresses with patterns of furious flowers flinging themselves around her waist. Her hair was the color of burned grass. She dyed it that way so that it would flare against her black skin.

Her parents abandoned her—her father had gone out for a packet of cigarettes and never came back, her mother had taken to the little white vials. The authorities found Dana locked in a cupboard, rake-thin, blind as the mice that scuttled in nursery rhymes, while her mother sat in the corner of the room and rocked on the balls of her toes, a bouquet of crack pipes around her feet. When she saw the badges, she just shrugged. *Take her, she ain't mine no more.*

Padraic pored over her files during his first week of work—she had taken swallows from bottles of Lysol, tried to hang herself with her shoelaces, defecated on a counselor's hairbrush, shorn off another girl's hair. At night, he would sit and read the file over and over, trying to make sense of the legion of quick signatures that cluttered the bottom of the pages. He would watch her in the common room, fingering the curtains. Once, in the back laundry room of the home, he saw her take a can of spray paint and begin to daub another girl's clothes. He talked to her about ordinary things—how she needed to learn to fold her towel neatly, control her temper, hold a pencil properly, stop biting her nails down to the quick. Sometimes he tried to describe colors to her, but the words broke down into a meaningless frenzy. He had a heavy caseload—seven boys and three girls—but Dana took up most of his time.

"You know what your name means?" he asked her one evening when they sat down to dinner.

"Nothing but a name."

"Well, yours is a bit different."

"Yeah sure."

"Okay," he said. He moved the fork around his plate, made a loud noise with it.

"No," she said suddenly. "Tell me."

Late into the evening he told her about Dana, the Irish goddess who was believed to have come from North Africa in ancient times. Dana was in charge of a tribe of druids, the Tuatha de Dannan, who landed on a fair May morning and conquered the country by ousting the Firbolgs, the men with the paunchy stomachs. She had magic that could control the sea, the mist, the sun, and the very sounds and shapes of the morning. They lived in a wild country where trees ran on one another's backs until they reached either ocean. Her tribe had made tunnels in vast mounds and built fairy forts down by the sea. They held four talismans of high power—the long sword and spear that had never been defeated, the stone of destiny, and the boiling cauldron for punishments.

"Ya mean they boiled people?"

"Eh, maybe."

"Cool." Dana was clanging her fork. "You ain't shittin' me?"

"Not a bit."

"She a witch, like?"

"Not really. If you want, I'll read you bits from a book," said Padraic.

"You talk funny," she said, chuckling.

For weeks afterward she threw questions at Padraic. How old was Dana? How did she die? Was she black? Was she blind? Did she wear colored clothes? They were questions he couldn't answer. Sometimes she would stalk around the hallways of the home, a towel thrown around her like a shawl, bumping into the doorways and the flower stands. She listened intently to the stories that he read to her. Once, he found in her notebook a drawing of a woman with four fluid faces meshed into one another, two of them sightless, two of them mesmerized by a river of yellow hair, all of them black. Padraic was amazed that she could draw like that.

On Saturday afternoons they walked toward the park. It was an area of furtive glances, shutters heavy over shop windows, basketball courts hemmed in with chicken wire, red brick tenement houses. They sat on wooden benches between a line of birch trees, whittling away the hours. Padraic talked to her of somewhere different, someplace where her namesake had been long ago. Dana imagined thick forests, boats made from the hides of cows, valleys where drizzling rain settled heavily on long grass.

One afternoon, after signing a welter of day-release passes, he took Dana home to meet Orla. Orla, a music scholar, played the cello for an hour. Dana fell asleep on the sofa. Later they brought her down to the sea, where she recoiled in fear at the touch of the cold water. Back up on the boardwalk, they huddled together under a long blue scarf. Then they rode the giant wooden roller coaster at Coney Island, and afterward, Dana begged them again and again to bring her back to the edge of the waves, which they did, all of them shivering in the slicing wind.

"How far is Ireland?" asked Dana.

"A long swim," he said.

"I'll wear a big coat," she said, bundling herself into the blue scarf.

"I hate it there now," he says to Orla as he sits on the side of the bed. "Ya should've seen it this morning when they heard they couldn't go to the wedding. Howling and lashing at the doors, they were. Charlie kicked the stereo to bits. Marcia tried to slit her friggin' wrists. Stephanie was calling me a sperm drinker."

"Good morning, and I love you too," says Orla. "Ya big sperm drinker."

Padraic laughs and tugs at his shoelaces. "Some day for a wedding, huh?"

"Ah, it's not too bad, as far as I can see," she says, climbing out of bed and walking over to the window to part the curtains, letting the light drone in on their tiny bedroom. "At least the sun is shining. We got married in the pissings of rain, remember?"

"Yeah, but we were normal and that was Ireland."

"Since when was Ireland normal?"

"Listen, close the curtains, would ya, love? I want to get a few hours kip. I'm knackered."

"Okay," says Orla. "I'm going to practice. Don't forget. The church at three o'clock."

"Last place in the world I want to be."

"You're giving her away."

"Exactly," he says, placing his glasses on the bedside table and pulling the sheets around his head.

The music from Orla's cello curls around the room and punctuates the roar of traffic outside. Padraic dozes with thoughts of Dana thundering in his head. He sees a cupboard and a little girl huddled under blankets, listening. He hears the poem that he sometimes quoted her when they walked in the park. *For the world's more full of weeping than you can understand.* He sees the small hand lost in a huge gold wedding band. He remembers strolling in the park with the echoing mythology of

Ireland. *Come away, stolen child.* Her tiny frame with the lop-sided walk, the shock of hair, the eyes lost in her head, the quiet anger. The afternoon when she left the home comes back to him in a flood of colors—she had packed her green mascara, braille books with blue covers, flowery skirts, a blue Yankees hat. As she gathered up the bits and pieces, he tried to convince her that there was another way, though he couldn't say what it was.

Waking from his nap he sees Orla at the stove, cooking lunch. He comes up behind her, puts his arms around her waist, as she watches the soup boil on the old stove.

"I really don't want to go," he whispers again.

She leans her head back on his shoulder.

"He's a freak, for crying out loud."

"Maybe she loves him."

"Yeah, sure."

"Listen, love," says Orla. "I graduate in six months. We can leave then. Go back to Ireland. Or you can get that job in Oregon."

"Ah, Jesus," he says, turning away from her. He shuffles over to the wall and stares at a print that hangs in a crooked frame. "I'm really tired of it, hon."

"Have a bowl of soup. You'll feel better at the wedding."

"I will in me arse."

"There too," she laughs.

"To hell with the soup. . . ."

"We already rented your suit."

"The place'll be full of freaks."

"You and your freaks," says Orla. "Would ya give it a break, for crying out loud?"

Dana met Will in the park. He sat in his wheelchair, wearing a long roll of gray beard that went down to his stomach, as if growing it in order to cover the place where he had no legs. He was more than twice her age. Paperback books about Vietnam curled dog-eared in his overcoat pockets. When he was eighteen his country had given him a haircut, a set of camos, a survival pack, and a machine gun and sent him off to the war. While he was in Saigon, Will's mother sent him a postcard saying that he was safe because he came from a good Christian family and he was "washed in the Blood of the Lamb." When he came home, in an airplane full of cripples and body bags, he wrote a note to his mother on the inside of a matchbox. He told her that, yeah, she was right but she spelled it wrong, although "Nam" just happened to rhyme.

Dana didn't tell Padraic about the man she met in the park. She began to get free rein and was allowed to walk down to the park on her own in the afternoons. She came back to the home, her face flushed. He wrote florid reports about her in the bottom of her file. She had begun to learn braille. He ordered books full of folklore from Ireland and read the stories. Under a special government program she learned how to walk with a guide dog. She drew more pictures of her own mythical Dana. They gained a more singular form, the colors vibrant and wild, the edges sharper, the lines less violent. Padraic began to wonder what might happen if she went to art college, and late in the evenings, he searched through brochures, flicking along through the photos of colleges smothered in autumn leaves, small New England spires rising in a background of hills, handsome men in overcoats and young women with healthy flushes in their cheeks. When he told her that he might be able to get her a scholarship, she just smiled and nodded her head.

He was in his office when another counselor told him that Dana was going to get married. He laughed at first. He had seen Will before, recognized him from the subway cars, where he regularly rattled a tin can, negotiating his chair through the crowd. There was a ferocious sadness in the veteran's eyes that made everyone on the carriage turn the other way while he spun along, clanging the tin can back and forth, held in gloves that had no fingers. He lived in a small hovel just down the road from the children's home, a black hole of other refugees and veterans, a place that seemed to invite a peculiar brand of bitterness.

When Padraic asked Dana about the wedding, she just raised her head, flung her fingers through her hair, and said that Will loved her, that nothing could stop her. They sat there, silent for a long time, the young girl fidgeting at her blouse, tears collecting at the edge of her cheeks. He went to the window, saying nothing as Dana shuffled out of the office. Later she asked him if he would give her away at the ceremony. He agreed but went for a long walk in the park and noticed for the first time how many eyes, blue and brown and green, were watching him as he threw small birch branches into the pond.

When Padraic and Orla arrive at the church, the pews are quite empty. Some of Will's friends are gathered up near the altar, leaning in over the wheelchair and fixing the groom's narrow, pale blue tie. Will is taking a furtive sip from a small bottle, wiping the sweat from his palms up and down his artificial legs. He has bought a new pair of fingerless gloves for the day. The priest seems drunk, stumbling out of the sacristy with a red stain on the front of his vestments. Vietnam vets with long hair and NO NUKE badges are running around with video cameras perched on their shoulders like rocket launchers.

A crowd of about thirty is gathered, including six of the blind kids from the home, brought along by two of the counselors. There are four guide dogs in the aisles, and one of them is barking loudly. Somebody must have changed their mind about the rule, but Padraic notices that neither Jimi nor Marcia nor Chocolate Charlie is there—they must have been put on room restriction after last night's fracas.

Orla kisses Padraic gently on the cheek and takes her seat near the front. He stands at the back of the church, waiting. He nods to a few people, shoves his hands deep into his pockets, mutters under his breath, then cranes his neck around to the parking lot. Dana eventually arrives in a battered Oldsmobile, long white ribbons in a frenzy on the hood. Her wedding dress is long and drawn tightly around her waist. Makeup is smudged around her eyes. Her hair is pulled into a bun at the back of her head. She holds a small bouquet of flowers. Padraic walks to the car and guides her by the elbow toward the church steps while a few guests snap their cameras.

"Padraic," she says. "Do I look okay?"

"You look great."

"Really?"

"Fabulous."

"Thanks."

"There's always time to change your mind, you know."

"You're like my father now," says Dana, leaning close to him. "You're not supposed to say things like that."

He draws her arm tightly to his. Someone plays the wedding song on a guitar, the tune high and twangy. For a moment he tries to describe the church to her, the stained-glass windows, the rows of shoulders, the guide dogs at the side of the pews, the priest swaying slightly in the center of the altar, but he knows she's not listening. He walks slowly with Dana up the center of the aisle as heads swivel. When the priest comes to take Dana up toward the altar, the smell of alcohol wafts through the air. She moves away easily, and Padraic sits down with a hefty thump beside Orla.

"Here we go with the show," he says.

He holds his wife's hand as the ceremony begins, but it's a twisted affair—the priest stumbling over the vows, the video cameras with their little red dots arranged like measles around the church, a dog wagging its tail gently in the aisle. The sermon is brief, the priest making a comparison to the wedding at Canaan. Will and Dana fumble with the rings, and Padraic watches as Will leans his bearded face upward toward the bride to kiss her. The guitar clangs out an old sixties hit.

"Let's get home," Padraic whispers as lightbulbs flash near the altar.

"What about the party?" whispers Orla.

"Thunderbird and dog biscuits."

"Jesus Christ, have some heart, will you?"

"Yeah, well."

"Get off your yeah-well arse and follow her down the aisle," she whispers, pushing at his ribcage.

He watches Will negotiate his wheelchair along the altar ramp. The veteran's beard has been groomed for the day. He catches Padraic's eye and winks for some reason. Padraic nods back. Dana's face is creased into a tremendous smile. She shuffles down the steps of the aisle with the help of the priest, then moves toward Will's wheelchair, where he's waiting. Instinctively she reaches out for the handles, finds them, and begins to push the chair along. The heels of Dana's shoes catch in her dress, but she regains her footing and begins to strut along the aisle, pushing the chair. A big laugh erupts around the church as she does a strange little skip in the air while pushing the chair.

Some of Will's friends at the entrance have ripped up small pieces of colored paper for confetti.

From behind, Padraic notices that Dana and Will seem joined together somehow as she wheels him along the outside ramp, the paper falling around their shoulders. "A little bit to the left," shouts Will, "watch out for the railings!" The colored paper falls around their shoulders. A bottle of champagne gets popped, and the priest reaches forward for a plastic glass. A crowd gathers around the newlyweds, and in the throng, Dana drops her bouquet of flowers. She whispers something in Will's ear and he gets her to spin the wheelchair around. She does it easily, calmly.

Padraic moves across to pick up the flowers, but he feels Will's hand grasp his.

"I'm all right, man," the veteran says.

"I'll just grab the flowers here."

"I'm all right," he says again.

"You sure?"

"Got the legs back."

"Yeah," says Padraic, unsure of what he means.

"And a pair of eyes for her."

"Yes, yeah."

"Ya know what I mean?"

"I know what you mean."

"We'll look after each other," says Will.

"Yeah."

"You know how it is."

"I do, yeah," says Padraic.

"All we're looking for now is a couple of skin grafts," says Will, gesturing toward Dana. He lets out a huge bellowing laugh. He turns around to Dana: "Did ya hear that? We're looking for skin grafts next."

Padraic steps back, embarrassed. He shoves his fists deep into his pockets. A flush rises up in his cheeks. He backs away from the crowd and watches as Will places the flowers back in Dana's hands. He has never really noticed before how attractive Dana is, how her fingers run delicately into long nails, how strands of hair run amok around her neck, how her skin gains color around her eyes. The crowd moves around Will and he reaches out, shakes hands, guides Dana's elbow toward other hands. Padraic wants to walk over to them to say something, anything, he's not sure what, something that suggests that strange things often happen, that certain moments are all too rare to be lost. But he simply stands there, rooted to his shadow.

He finds himself thinking of the children's home—Chocolate Charlie lounging around by the smashed stereo, balancing a soccer ball on his foot; Marcia watching the thin scab grow again on her wrist; Jimi hiding a pair of matches under his pillow. Tomorrow morning they'll crowd around him, asking a million questions about the wedding. Toast will be thrown in the dining room. A pair of socks will be lost in the laundry. A fight will break out in the cafeteria. All the ordinary bits and pieces of seconds, minutes, hours, will clatter on, regardless.

Padraic scuffles at his shoes, noticing that he forgot to polish them. He looks for Orla in the crowd. He sees her at the edge of the church steps, two plastic glasses in her hands. He pulls his hands from his pockets and moves toward her. She raises the champagne in the air and he nods back, slowly at first, like a bird beginning to peck at a few crumbs lying on the ground.

STEP WE GAILY,

ON WE GO

Give life long enough and it'll solve all your problems, even the problem of being alive. Should write that one on the stairwell, he chuckles to himself as he shuffles down the rat-gray steps of the apartment complex. He walks slowly, his big shoulders pitching back and forth in the folds of an old brown overcoat. Thick fists, blotched here and there with liver spots, pop out from the cuffs and a magenta handkerchief sprouts from the breast pocket. Beads of sweat gather beneath the peak of his flat tweed cap as he negotiates the corner on the third floor. Damn, he thinks, it's hot under this whole rigout.

As he walks down the steps—past the familiar, rude graffiti—three teenaged boys, wearing their black baseball hats turned backward, point at him and throw their fists up at the sky. He winks at them and they laugh, then they turn away, punching each other on the shoulders and imitating his slouch. Nothing that a good clip on the ear wouldn't solve. He smiles, takes the hanky from his pocket, and mops his brow. Farther down the stairwell an old woman with a shopping bag full of cauliflowers passes him, muttering something about the weather and the terrible things it does to vegetables. He tips his hat to her, then bows as a pretty little girl skips past him, hands clutching the bottom of her dress, carrying crayons in the upturned folds. Hope to God it's not her that's writing these sloppy swirls of graffiti on the walls.

He pauses on the third floor and reads: *When did the black man learn to walk?* Beneath it: *When the white man invented the wheelbarrow.* Beneath that: *Eat shit, honky motherfucker.* A strange one that, because surely not even the front of a wheelbarrow would be too comfortable, certainly not for a codger his age. There was, however, a rich eccentric gentleman he once heard of who was designing his garden in the dun-and-green Wicklow hills, far away. The gentleman was known to have his gardeners wheel him around in a big brown barrow, while he sat in the damn thing and drank tea. From a saucer. The excuse for the gentleman's transport was that he was afflicted with brucelosis, gotten when he pricked his finger on a thorny rose bush, then put his hands in some composted horse manure. Deep shit, to paraphrase the graffiti.

He pauses for a moment and leans against the railing, pensive. Isn't it a strange word that? Motherfucker. And a violent one too. Not at all poetic. Awful, in fact. But used all the time in these parts.

He himself has been called it, not in derision but in a curiously lovely way, when in the deep-shadowed corners late at night he can hear them make bets that the old Irish mother-fucker could probably still throw a punch or two. And a punch or two they would deserve, but for the fact that he has been so long a part of the scenery that he understands that a mother-fucker, among the black boys anyway, is a brother. The Mexicans here are quiet and furtive, the young ones standing around with hands in pockets, and they are seldom heard, in his ears anyway, to use the word. It's the white ones—the trash, as they say—who use it most vindictively.

Mopping his brow once more, he moves away from the railing toward the second-floor steps.

Jesus, it's a long way to the laundromat in heat like this. *And longer every day, though your steps be heavy you'll trot lightly along the way.* A grand tune that. One that he used to sing long ago. A lovely melody to it. A damnsight removed from this graffiti, that's for sure. Less imaginative every day, he rues, though he stops by his favorite aphorism, down in the alcove of the second floor, where some poor gouger has left a puddle of urine. *Women of the world rise up out of the bed of your oppressors . . . and go make breakfast.* He tips his tweed cap to that one. Sausages and rashers, please, Juanita, and throw in a dollop of that fine blood pudding you have hanging over the stove. When you're finished the washing up, love, roll out the wheelbarrow and we'll go for a waltz around the city where all of America sludges down to the sea. He laughs to himself. If Juanita heard him say that, she'd be outraged. She'd be on her bike, off home to Hollywood. Never in her life has she made breakfast for him. And not damn likely to either. Gorgeous as she is, Juanita is a ferocious woman. A temper on her to calm the seven seas. And a voicebox that's been known to boom. And her, so small and sweet and delicate. Juanita. Up and away, Flaherty, me boy. No time for all this dilly-dallying.

He moves away from the puddle of pee, holding his nose— broken many times—and wonders who it was wrote the little gem of graffiti. The man who tapped his kidney? Surely not. No fountains of helicon for him. The little girl with the up- turned dress full of crayons? You never know these days—he has heard that they installed metal detectors last week in what they call the junior high. An appropriate enough name since the kids around here are known to have a fondness for drugs. And guns. At the far end of the complex there is another slo- gan. *Guns 'n Roses.* For that there surely is no logic.

He shuffles down toward the ground floor through all the words. *Eat the homeless. Johnny X is hung like a horse. Leroy is sprunger than a mofo.* Johnny X, it seems, has no problems. But give life long enough, Leroy, and it will solve them all. These drugs, he knows, are a terrible thing. Far away, *the crack* is a phrase for a good time. Not here. He has seen boys in this place—boys he taught to jab at the sky—swapping food stamps for little white bags. Leroy and Johnny X might well have been among them, though the names in his head tend to collide with one another.

There had been one boy, however, who made it out of here—Tyrone Jacobs, who is due to fight in Madison Square Garden tonight. Twelve years ago he was teaching Tyrone how to punch, the boy's bog-black skin shining with sweat day after day after day in the hot sun spitting down in the complex's courtyard. Keep your elbows tucked, young Tyrone. Wait for the hole. Spare the right. Dance a little. Jab. Atta boy. Move away. Dance. Throw that shoulder. Fake. He pauses and wonders if Tyrone will remember the right moves, if they'll put a prize around his rib-tight body, a belt that he himself never won in the heavyweight division. For a moment he lets himself think of the Caffola fight and mustard oil. September 9, 1938. A bitter thought. Then he lets a little jab fly at the sky and almost loses his footing on the stairs.

In a great poem there was a man who tripped lightly along the ledge of a deep ravine where passions were pledged. And isn't that the truth? Down the steps with a sprightly leap, he emerges from the complex into the New Orleans sun. He shades his eyes with his cap and looks around. A dirge of girls, one pregnant, prop up the streetcorner flower shop. They begin to giggle when they see him. He fingers his brown belted overcoat. It's hotter than a July bride out here, by God, but he'll need the overcoat when he gets to the laundromat. Part of the camouflage.

He recognizes a flouncy, frilly blue blouse on the pregnant girl, a blouse that Juanita decided she didn't like a few months ago. When Juanita—who can be awful finicky—doesn't like a piece of clothing, she flat out refuses to wear it again. So one day last month, after a year of acquiring new clothes for her, he decided to put them to some use. Give them to others who might wear them. Late one night, he furtively left his apartment with the blouse and hung it on the doorknob of Mrs. Jackson's place. The next morning he watched the old woman come out onto the balcony. When she found the blue beauty on the doorknob, there was a smile splayed on her face that painted the whole world well.

After Mrs. Jackson, there had been a welter of Juanita's clothes hung out on doorknobs all over the complex. Juanita doesn't mind. She doesn't even know about it. Nobody knows. But people around here need them, by God. There are Maid Marians everywhere, though the forest is paved over and gray.

"Good morning, Miss Jackson," he says, nodding to the young girl with the bun—or the buns—in the oven. Both perhaps. She is suitably startled that he knows her name, and he smiles, then winks. "It's a grand day."

"Yessir," the girl fumbles.

"Lovely flowers," he says, pointing at the window.

"Yessir, lovely flowers."

Ah, but he didn't mean to embarrass her like that, winking at a young one who's up the Swannee. He shuffles on past the shop. Flaherty, son, keep your tongue in your mouth, you damn fool. He was always the one for embarrassing women. When he did the cabarets with Juanita in the fifties, one night they were walking down by the Liffey and saw two men huddled in the shadows of Merchant's Arch. Dublin wasn't renowned for its homosexuals, and he'd sung, in a gorgeous voice: *In Dublin's fair city, where the boys are so pretty, I first set my eyes on sweet Michael Malone, where he wheels his wheelbarrow through the streets broad and narrow, crying muscle out your cockles alive-alive-o.* The two men, furious at the ditty, made a move for him, their fists clenched tight. But when they saw his shoulders, and perhaps remembered his photographs in the newspapers—"the phonic pugilist" was what the *Evening Mail* dubbed him—the two men turned the other way. Juanita was embarrassed, as well she should have been. She said that no matter what sexual persuasion—sheep or shearers—they should be allowed to do what they want. Juanita is small and frail but has a mouth on her as sharp as a new blade of grass.

Stopping at the traffic lights, he looks over his shoulder. The poor young girl back there by the flower shop, waiting for roses and proper pledged passions. Perhaps he'll leave another one of Juanita's blouses on her mother's doorknob one of these days. One big enough for the baby, mind you. But, Jesus, aren't wheelbarrows and roses—and even that awful thought, mother-fuckers—coming up a fierce lot today? Must be the heat. Hotter than a jalapeño in hell. That's Juanita's phrase. She loves peppers. That it was too, hotter than a jalapeño in heaven or hell or anywhere else the night of the Caffola fight. September 9, 1938. Mustard oil.

He can hear the roar of the traffic from the I-10 highway and the rumble of a trolley coming up Carrollton Avenue. He stands at the edge of the wide road, waiting to walk. To cross the road in this country a man needs a damn Ph.D. in civil engineering. And a body on you like a racehorse. Johnny X would do well here. He waits for the little green man—not the same one you find on a can of beans—to flash on. And remembers that he's hungry. But onward we go. "We should go forth," as an American poet once said, "on the shortest journey, in the spirit of undying adventure, never to return." But what would Thoreau know? He lived in a cabin by a lake all on his own. Flaherty, me boy, you've been reading too many books, and if you don't get across the damn road quickly, the green man will be red and you'll be dead. Good Christ. This rhyming. It must be the heat. An imaginative man would have said: wooden overcoat. And left the rhymes to reason.

He crosses the road, stops, and surveys the traffic, then breathes deeply. Not as much in the lungs as there used to be. But it isn't too far now to the laundromat, thank Jesus. *Step we gaily, on we go, heel for heel and toe for toe, arm in arm and row in row, off for Marie's wedding.* His favorite song, no matter who the hell Marie is or was. Singing, he undoes the big brown belt of his overcoat. What will Juanita like? A flowery skirt? A pink blouse with tassels? Another flouncy blue number like Miss Jackson was wearing? No. What's in order, he thinks, is something that will fit her like the sky fits the earth. That much at least she deserves. Today is a very special anniversary—July 9th, 1992. Juanita is still as beautiful as ever, and she deserves something special.

He sees a young boy walking by the fried chicken shop, with his hair sticking up in little shafts of electrocuted pink. What in the world has become of hairstyles? When we were boys, in Lisdoonvarna, the hair gel came in two-penny bottles. We would part our hair down the middle and it would shine in the moonlight on the way home from the dancehall.

Those were the days. Indeed. He left for America on the Washington cruiser, swearing to Ireland that he would come home Heavyweight Champion of the World. Days of cowlicks and curls. It was the Great Depression, he remembers, and unemployed men hung around, warming their hands over hot barrels on the dockside in Cobh, eating pigeon sandwiches. Some among them had mouths festered from eating nettles. Hard times, and even back then, America was the place to go. Lachrymose young girls sold daffodils so they could buy tickets. Boys stood up high on the backs of dung carts, looking out to sea, dreaming. Bilious crowds watched the white of the waves while the ships foghorned a song of exile. Getting on the boat, standing on the deck, he sang *Ireland, I love you, a Chusla Mo Chroí*, love of my heart. As the boat pulled away he remembered his parents, who died when he was just fifteen. His mother, a hard woman, a disarray of beauty, maps of the west wrinkled on her skin. His father, an American who had come to Ireland after the agonies of the Great War, a man who learned how to farm and make soil among the barren rocks, a hard-working man, honest and doomed.

He stands at the side of Carrollton Avenue, feeling the heat hammer down from the southern sky. He wipes his overcoat sleeve across his wet brow.

They had given their son thick hands, hands that won fights all over Ireland, even illegal bouts in the grassy wild meadows. That day, when he stood on the ship's bow in Cobh, the world stretched out in front of him. In his first eight months, in dingy little New York halls, he put away three journeymen heavyweights. Always sang a song after each of the bouts. Fell in love with Juanita when she came with a movie director to one of the fights. She sat there in the third row, her hair as wild and as long as kelp. That night he took her to the fanciest restaurant in town, and she kissed the top of his eye where he'd been cut.

One victory flew into another. In the dressing room Juanita took to massaging his shoulders like some women take to kneading bread. Reporters in wide hats began to take notice. A photo appeared in the papers of him and Juanita swapping wedding bands. Him decked out in a white tuxedo jacket, her in the finest taffeta, a bouquet of white flowers in her dark hair. That was the week before the big fight. September 9, 1938. If he could beat Caffola he would go on to the big time. Mustard oil. Blinded him good-oh. Juanita in the ring, smoothing back his hair, saying it'll be all right, Danny, it'll be all right, there'll be another chance. His hair falling back again, down over his eyes.

And now it has fallen away in furrows, though he has his little flat cap on to cover up the bald spots. But onward to the washing machines. Hup, two, three. Enough of years gone by. *Put it behind you, make it anew, put it behind you, and things'll come true.* There was a comeback after Caffola, and he was swearing to reporters that if he got the chance, he would take on Buddy Baer and the Brown Bomber in the same ring. But he had fallen easily to a no-hoper from the bowels of Brooklyn. *A Chusla Mo Chroí.* Love of my heart and, sweet Jesus, would you ever get a move on? Step we gaily, on we go. The sun'll be down before I get home to Juanita.

She brought him to Hollywood where she was making some

movies. But there wasn't enough call for a Mexican girl. Beautiful as she was, and a voice so gorgeous she sounded like she had a wren in her throat, they terminated her contract. The couple stood on the deck of another boat, combing the waves in an easterly way. They sang together in the smoky cabarets of Ireland and Britain where men in zoot suits wet the tip ends of cigars with lascivious tongues and stared. But the cabarets closed, eyelids on an era. Then it was back to America, where their bodies gave way, but the social welfare checks dropped regularly enough to keep them happy. And a million years lived in between all that. Things he's forgotten. *In the meantime, in between time, ain't we got fun?* Put it behind you. Make it anew. But how the hell can you put it behind you, how in God's name can you make it anew? Christ but the heat is doing strange things to my head. Onward. Away.

"Something chasing you, Mr. Flaherty?" It's Clarence Le-Blanc, that sly-eyed bastard in trousers too tight even for his thin legs, thirty years old maybe, who works as the rent collector in the complex. He's coming out of the 7-Eleven with a packet of cigarettes in his long thin black hands. LeBlanc is often seen scrubbing the graffiti from the walls. A Philistine if ever there was one. And always that nasty upturned lip when he knocks on the door to collect the rent.

"Chasing me?" said Flaherty.

"Seems like you in a hurry."

"Off to the laundromat."

"Doing you some washing?"

"I am."

"Funny, I don't see no clothes." LeBlanc has that glint in his eye.

"I left them yonder this morning."

"You best watch out."

"Why's that?"

"Somebody been stealing clothes down there. Believe it must be one of the young guys from our complex."

"It's a terrible thing these days, the thievery," says Flaherty. "Are ya going to watch the fight on TV tonight?"

"Hanging them on doorknobs," says LeBlanc.

"Young whippersnappers. Can't trust a soul these days." He shuffles his feet and balls up his fists. "Tyrone is fighting in the Garden." A slow roundhouse comes from the shoulders, hitting air, and he smiles.

"I don't follow boxing, Mr. Flaherty," says LeBlanc, lighting up a cigarette. "You see anything strange, you let me know."

"Indeed I will."

He curses softly to himself as LeBlanc moves away. The cat's out of the bag and meowing at the man in the moon. He hunkers into his coat, feeling the sweat roll down his armpits. The traffic thunders on in his ears as he negotiates a couple of potholes. He squints and feels almost dizzy. For a moment he sees his mother bent over the sink, scrubbing some blood from the collar of a white shirt. His father outside, hanging a sandbag from a chestnut tree, shouting at him to get ready for practice. Juanita leaning into the microphone, hair thrown back, eyes brown and deep. Tyrone dancing in the middle of a ring.

He skirts in past a couple of cars, negotiates the curb, tongues a bead of sweat off his lip, stands for a moment and watches the clouds scud along over the city, then opens the laundromat door. He hears the whirl of washing machines. The pink neon throws patches of light down on his brown overcoat. A plane on a video game crash lands in the corner. The Coke machine is taped with a huge OUT OF ORDER sign. He sits down on the plastic chair, wheezing softly, takes off his flat cap, places it on the seat beside him, and looks around some more.

It's the wealthy women who come to this place. Well, not exactly wealthy, but better off than those in the complex. A dollar a load here. The machines are shiny-new and the hands that open them are mostly white. Kids from the university come here, in cherry-red convertibles. Spoiled rotten, the whole lot of them. Always throw in their laundry and come back half an hour later. At the other laundromat, east of the complex, it's only fifty cents a load and everyone stays, watching their clothes like nervous birds over crumbs.

There are only three women in the laundromat now, two at the far end, heads deep in magazines, and one—a real fancy-pants with blond hair and pink lipstick—loading a huge blue bag of clothes into washers number three, four, and five. Each time she lifts something out of her laundry bag she holds it up to the light and examines it very carefully. A set of sheets. Towels. Socks. T-shirts. Some underwear tucked into machine number four very quickly. A nightshirt. Washcloth. Then Fancypants takes out a pair of ragged Levis, followed by a couple of skirts.

101

Juanita, unfortunately, wouldn't look good in any of them. She has always been the one for great style, something a little modest but show-offy all the same. When she went to the fights it was always a magenta dress. In the cabarets it was often that glittery sequined number, grassy green. On the boats, back and forth across oceans, it was always something the color of the sea. He shuffles his feet. Juanita. My Juanita. Love of my heart and oh, would you look at that!

Fancypants is lifting up a white shirt with lacy see-through sleeves. Blue frills on the collar. A gorgeous piece of work. She frowns, perhaps considering whether she should get it dry-cleaned or not. It's the perfect size. A fan whirls above his head. He sweats and watches Fancypants. She fidgets for a moment, then puts the white blouse in machine number five. His heart skips a tune. He watches Fancypants take out a bottle of expensive detergent. The way she pours, you can tell she's rich. She probably won't even notice that the damn thing's gone. And on her way out the door she doesn't even smile at him.

He looks around. Rubs his hands together. Smacks his lips. Now's my chance. The other two still have their heads in their magazines. The place smells like a hospital. Too clean altogether. Not a bit of graffiti on the walls. No soul whatsoever. He starts to hum: *Ol' buttermilk sky, I'm a telling you why, now you know, keep it in mind tonight, are you going to be mellow tonight?* As Fancypants's car moves away, he walks toward machine number five. He lifts the lid quickly. Fingers shaking. Rummages. Finds it. Water spurting down onto his thick hands. He takes the white blouse and tucks it under his overcoat. *Can't you see my little donkey and me, we're as happy as a Christmas tree, heading for the one I love, the one I love.* Whistles softly to himself. It will be a little wet, a small spot of blue detergent on the sleeve, but who cares? Juanita will love it. *Gonna poppa the question, that question, do you darling, do you do? It'll be easy so easy if I can only bank on you.* He feels the wetness of the blouse beginning to seep against his own shirt. He lets a little smile fly from his lips and shuffles out the laundromat door. Christ, he thinks, but it sure is a hot one today.

He sits in the leather chair that the good folks down at Saint Vincent de Paul's gave him for a dollar. The room is small and cluttered and full of silence. On the mantelpiece there is a picture of him as a young man in red gloves. His skin is drawn tightly over muscles. Those were the days. A cowlick hanging happily over green eyes. A pair of silk shorts hangs beside the photo. A couple of trophies nearby. Sheets on the bed are crumpled. Above the bed is a picture of Juanita, her hair threaded down her back, like the girl in the song with her hair hung over her shoulder. Beautiful. My Juanita. Books of poetry talk to one another on the floor. A TV spits gray. A kettle boils. The cupboard at the end of the room is full of women's clothes. Blouses. Dresses. Skirts. Scarves. It's getting choc-a-bloc in there. He must get busy with the doorknobs. He smiles to himself.

Right in front of him, on a coat hanger dangling from the

103

lampshade, is the white blouse with the blue frills. He gets up slowly from the leather chair, wheezes, reaches out, and touches the sleeves that dangle in the air. Runs his arms along the collar. Then presses his face against the blouse, holding it, breathing in deeply, smiling.

"Juanita," he says softly. "Juanita, my love, you look absolutely gorgeous."

.

On down past the graffiti again, hurrying this time. He has remembered that he left his tweed cap on one of the plastic chairs back in the laundromat. Hope to Christ that Fancypants isn't still there. It's been an hour and a half, and surely the tumble dryer has finished now and she's off and away, oblivious. Get a move on now, Flaherty. Step we quickly on we go. No gaiety now. And sure isn't gaiety something altogether unfashionable these days, unless you live in the French Quarter? There's some graffiti on the walls about homosexuals, but nothing as good as the cocking out of muscles, alive-alive-o. Hup two.

Juanita will be hopping mad if he isn't home in time for the tea that she has boiling on the stove. And even madder if she finds out that he's lost his hat. She bought it for him in Clery's in Dublin back in the fifties, when money was round and made to roll. They walked out onto O'Connell Street in the drizzling rain, and she pulled it delicately over his black curls. Said it made him look like a leprechaun. Leprecorny perhaps. She laughed. People stared as they walked. A tall brick of a man and a tiny Mexican girl, fitting together like a hand in a glove. Sauntering down the quays, stopping in bookshops. The Liffey tossing down to the sea, barges bound from the brewery, pigeons quarelling over bread, motor cars beeping at tinkers in horse carts. Kissing Juanita under the blue awning of an antique store. *Ah, she looked so sweet from her two bare feet to the sheen of her lush brown hair.* Hup two. On you go, with a song in your heart. Gotta get the damn hat back.

He almost falls on the steps near his favorite piece of graffiti, grazing his hand as he uses it to prevent a fall. Rise up out of the bed of your oppressors, he mutters to himself. Quickly now. Hup two three four.

He negotiates the steps, wheezes out onto Carrollton Avenue, and looks up the street. Damnblast and bugger it. There's Clarence LeBlanc leaning his skinny legs up against the wall, chatting with Miss Jackson. Maybe he's the one who got her up the Swannee. *Howiloveya, howiloveya, my dear ol' Swannee.* He hopes not. LeBlanc couldn't squire anything but a long lanky drink of bogwater. Perhaps, however, when Juanita decides that she's worn the white blouse with the blue frills long enough, he'll give it to the pregnant girl, though it might be a little tight around her belly. He moves to tip his hat to them, then remembers that it isn't there. A man without his hat is like a pig with a gold ring in its nose. Down the road, alongside the clutter and clang of cars. LeBlanc is shouting something behind him, but he pretends he doesn't hear. Quickly now, Flaherty. On your toes. No time for graffiti.

Down past the flower shop, the little green man flashing, cars beeping, the clammy roar of a hot New Orleans afternoon. Thirty damn years of living in this town and never once was I able to cross the damn road in time. Past the chicken shop, past the bank. The neon sign flickers. 4:31 P.M. 94 degrees. Jalapeño time. Upwards, Flaherty. Away. May your ways be merry and your paths be few. Hup two. Christ. Still rhyming. Hot. Hot. Hot. He takes off his overcoat as he shuffles and tucks it under his arm when he gets to the parking lot of the laundromat. Negotiates a couple of potholes. Give me a ring with ropes and I still could dance. And, sweet Jesus, there in all her glory, a little bit bemused, by washing machine number six, is Fancypants.

He stalls in the parking lot, wondering. But Fancypants couldn't have a clue. Probably hasn't even noticed the missing shirt. Have to get the cap back anyway. A man's gotta do. Juanita will be hopping mad if I lose it. She adores that hat. He shuffles toward the door, keeping his eyes down. Hup two. On the seat nearest the door, he catches a glimpse of his gray tweed. Hallelujah and hail to the king. Grand job, Nora, as the saying goes. Nora being the girl that the bold Sean O'Casey left behind. He chuckles to himself. Here comes the Playboy of the Western World. Or was that Mr. Synge? Onward. Away. On yer bike. Quickly.

He looks up and notices that Fancypants is watching him. Uh-oh. He smiles at her as he picks up the hat. "Fierce hot today isn't it?" he says to her.

"What?" She moves out from around the back of the machines. "Yes. Well. Excuse me, sir, did you happen, by any chance, to, like, see somebody in here?"

"Not a soul. I just forgot my hat."

"I misplaced a blouse."

"Sorry to hear that. Well, I must be on my way. Juanita expects me home. She has the tea on."

"Excuse me?" says Fancypants.

"My wife. She'll be angry as all get-out if I lose my cap. I left my cap here."

"Oh," says Fancypants.

"Had to run all the way here. Still have it in my lungs, all the same. Used to run six miles a day. Way back when."

"I see. But you didn't happen to see anyone in . . ."

"Devil a soul. There were two women when I left. Now that you mention it."

"Did they go to that washing machine?" Fancypants points over toward number five.

"Not that I know of." With his back to the door he hears someone enter the laundromat. He doesn't turn around, just stands, watching Fancypants. "I hear there's been some thievery going on all the same," he says. "It's a terrible thing. Can't trust a soul these days. All the young ones are into drugs. No wonder they call it the junior high."

"Sorry?"

"The school and the drugs. No wonder they call it the junior high."

"My boyfriend gave it to me," says Fancypants, scratching her head. "It's no big deal really, I suppose. Just sentimental value."

A finger of guilt doing circles in his stomach. He touches his hat, pulls the flap down over his eyes. "Well, dear," he says, "I must be on me way. Awful sorry about the blouse. But I must get on home. My wife'll be fussing and fuming."

"Thank you," she says. "Sorry for delaying you." Oh, but she's awful nice, this Fancypants with her twirly blond hair and her lipstick. Maybe he should run on home and retrieve it for her. Juanita wasn't mad keen about it anyway. Didn't like the blue frills.

A thick gravelly voice comes from behind his shoulder. "Whose wife might that be, Mr. Flaherty?"

He turns. Jesus, Mary, and Joseph, what the hell is Clarence LeBlanc doing in here? Standing by the door, the lanky drink-of-water has a vicious sneer on his face. "Flaherty, you don't have a wife."

A buckle of knees, a heart thump. Where the hell did LeBlanc appear from?

"Whose wife are we talking about?" LeBlanc says again.

"I have to go home, dear," he says to Fancypants. "Excuse me, now. The tea's boiling. I hope you find the blouse."

"Whose wife, Mr. Flaherty?" LeBlanc stands with his arms stretched out, blocking the doorway. "You don't have no wife."

"If you'll kindly excuse me," he says to LeBlanc. Behind him he can hear Fancypants stuttering something. "Are you missing something, ma'am?" says LeBlanc to Fancypants.

"Just a blouse. I misplaced a blouse. It's no big deal."

"You don't happen to know anything about the young lady's blouse, do you, Mr. Flaherty?"

"Not a thing. Could you excuse me?" He puts his hand on LeBlanc's shoulder to get beyond him. Christ, but it's hot. LeBlanc pushes him in the chest. He stumbles backward.

"Pervert," hisses LeBlanc. "You a pervert, Flaherty. Stealing women's clothes. I been knowing it all along."

The day she left he stood in front of the door, just like this, except he was the one blocking. So many years ago. Another steaming New Orleans day. Her hair was ashy and ferocious that afternoon, her skin wallpapered with grief. I'll sing to you, Juanita. You've sung enough, and I've heard them all before. I'll make it anew. Get out of my way please, Danny. I'll try harder. No. I'll go with you. I'm going where you can't find me. Why? I've had enough. Of what? Of everything. I don't understand. And you never will. He tried to touch her hair. She pulled back. There were lines on her face now. They were both so much older than the moon they had sung to. When will you be back, Juanita? When the sun comes up in the west, Danny, and maybe even a few days after that. Then him leaning against the door, watching her go.

That was July 9, 1967. Twenty-five years ago to the day. The summer of love they called it. A bad name, and not true at all. The cabarets, the bells, the canvas, the movies, the sheer theater of it all, the wonder—gone. He had fallen to Caffola. She had fallen, not unlike a silver goddess. Their voices had fallen too. Down somewhere deep in the belly of memory. And the hope as well. The courtyard complex was gray as granite that day when she left. She slipped out the door and he thought of home, far away, far away. The garden of rock. The limestone that lets the water seep through. The turloughs with their disappearing water. The strangely colored flowers. She would be back. He would wait. Granite was impermeable. That he had learned. Granite doesn't let water through.

It's a slow punch, an old man's roundhouse, and LeBlanc should have seen it coming. But it lands crisply on his jaw, sweetly, no fear, like old times. A good healthy crunch through his fingers. If only he could have hit Caffola like that before the bastard smeared mustard oil on his gloves. September 9, 1938. Falling sideways with a thud. Referee calling the count. Juanita up on the ropes. Shouting in Spanish. Danny get up. Get up. Looking like she had four eyes. Everything swirling. Stumbling on the ropes. Finished. Gone. *A Chusla Mo Chroí*, and it's all over now, Danny boy.

LeBlanc falls the same way, splayed across the plastic chairs, a pack of cigarettes tumbling from his shirt pocket. Fancypants lets out a little yelp. And it's out the door, running.

Over a pothole and far away. Far away, far away. And a glance behind. Though your steps be heavy, you'll trot lightly along the way. Hup two, Flaherty. On home to Juanita. Tea's ready. A dab of milk and a spoonful of sugar, dearest. He looks over his shoulder, breathing heavily. LeBlanc is behind him now, one hundred yards to the rear, blood streaming from his mouth. Oh, a great punch that one. Hit him good-oh. Yessir. Put me in the Hall of Fame. Hang my gloves beside those of the Brown Bomber. A fabulous punch indeed.

LeBlanc is roaring something obscene behind him. Is nothing sacred at all? But he's gaining awful fast. Past the bank. Alongside the chicken shop. If I can make the flashing green man, he thinks, I'll be home free. Myself and Juanita can watch Tyrone on the TV, flinging his lovely fists at the sky. Then I'll steal out tonight and leave Miss Jackson a blouse. White with blue frills. Awful nice that blouse, but Juanita just didn't like it. Women. They're so shagging fin-icky. Run, Flaherty, run. Run. Look at the trouble they get you into. He looks over his shoulder again. LeBlanc is only forty yards away. Christ, the boy is fast. Into the traffic he darts. Hup two three. LeBlanc is screaming awful loud. Well, fuck you too, my bonnie boy. A screech of tires. Thank jaysus that green man isn't red. Onwards. Upwards. Away. Quick, quick, quick. He'll never catch me. Along the side-walk.

Juanita, when I'm home make it two spoonfuls of sugar. To

help the medicine go down. Then I'll sing you the finest song you ever heard. Past the flower shop. He makes it to the steps of the complex, then turns around. LeBlanc is right there. He looks up the stairwell, toward the graffiti, then back at LeBlanc again. Gaining fast. Awful, awful fast. Fists clenched. Sneer on his face. Eyes like scythes. Up the steps. One two three. Alongside the graffiti. One two. Panting. One. One. Two. Leaning against the wall. Gasping now. Looking backward. LeBlanc reaching out for him.

Christ, he thinks, with a huge skip of the heart, buy that bastard a wheelbarrow.

A WORD IN EDGEWISE

L ook at you and a smile on you like the cracked vase that
Mammy kept in the kitchen cupboard. The flowery one.
With the downward chink, like an upturned smile. Daisies, I
think they were, with little yellow figurines leaping all the way
through them. A poet one time wrote about a vase, or an urn,
and something about beauty and truth. A damnsight we were
away from truth those nights, hai? You jumping around the
dancehall like a prayer in an air raid, your hair running wild and
frothy all around your shoulders. Weren't we a sight? You,
sneaking off down to the town square with Francis Hogan, the
only lad in town with a motorcar, done up to the nines, your
mascara on, your ginger hair flying. Him with his elbow hung
out the window, smoking, his curls all slicked back with oil.
What a sight! Me sitting sidesaddle on Tommy Coyne's red
tractor, chugging our way out to the fields behind the elder-
berry forest, going to make hay, as we say. Wasn't that the time
of it? A tube of lipstick was a precious thing in those days.

The young ones nowadays, they don't think we were up to it

at all. Here we are, getting letters from the grandkids, all over the globe, and I'll be bowled arse-over-backward if they think we ever misbehaved. Did I tell you about the letter I got a few days ago from young Fiachra in Amsterdam? Tells me the tulips look lovely in spring. I ask you, eighteen years old and he wants me to think he's looking at the tulips! Not only making hay, but he's probably threshing the damn stuff as well. They do that sort of thing in Amsterdam. It's a long way from Tipperary. Or a long way to tip her hairy, as Tommy Coyne was once heard to sing, outside the dancehall, sitting on the back of his tractor. Holy God! I don't mean to be rude, Moira, but I kid you not. Sitting on the back of his tractor with the blackberry juice on his teeth and his hair in a cowlick: *It's a long way to tip her hairy, it's a long way to go, it's a long way to tip the hairy of the sweetest gal I know, Godblessher.* God bless us and save us! It's the years, Moira. I'm wont to ramble, as you well know.

Lipstick. Cleanser. Mascara. A touch of rouge. Eyeliner. The whole nine yards. We'll have you smiling yet. Come off it now, of course we will. Anyway, didn't Da get into awful conniptions over me knocking the kitchen teapot over the night we came in from the dancehall? Smashed on the kitchen tiles, it did, with an awful racket. Ricocheting through the house. Us standing there, the smell of drink on our breaths, in those blue dresses sent from Paris by Aunt Orla. Him as big as the Rathcannon elk, roaring: "Weren't you two supposed to be home by ten?" And both of us stealing out again and sitting in the vegetable patch near the barn, laughing our heads off until the sun was just about up. And us just smearing the makeup all over

each other's faces! We must have looked awful stupid—sitting
in a straggle of turnips, wearing fancy blue dresses.

Funny thing is, these days we're always asleep by ten, let
alone home. Time has a curious way. But that's how it goes
isn't it? Da away and beyond, God rest his soul. Mammy too.
And Aunt Orla with her. Sure, who knows where even Tommy
Coyne is these days? Up and left for Australia long before it was
the fashionable place to go. Remember all those jokes about
Tommy Coyne and sheep! Me oh my. Hold on a minute now,
Moira, and the first thing I'm going to do is put on a little
cleanser. New stuff I got from Max Factor. Lovely clean smell
to it, isn't there?

Good God Almighty! But haven't we been doing this since
the Lord knows when? Remember the times when we were
toddlers and Mammy would be on the way out to the pub with
Da? He'd be there, all big-boned, at the end of the stairs, in his
blue suit, shouting at her to hurry on. And Mammy always so
meticulous with the lipstick, wasn't she? Forever licking her
tongue over her teeth, head cocked sideways, staring at herself.
I suppose that's where we got it from. Us glued wide-eyed on
either side of her. Then us sneaking out of bed when they were
gone, to sit in front of the big oak mirror and smear it all over
our lips, trying her hats on, and making curtseys in the middle
of the room. Damn it, anyway, but weren't we the holy terrors!
Remember that night when we took what's-her-name, the cat,
you know, oh, whatsit? Luna! That's it. Luna. Remember we
took her and covered her with rouge, put mascara on the
whiskers, perfumed behind the poor thing's ears and dressed

her in a rag of old satin? That little wag of a tail coming out the back. That poor cat hissing around the house, like something possessed. Hiding under the bed. The hat you made for her with Da's cigarette packs. The things we remember.

Anyway, talking of teapots, strange the way things change, isn't it? Used to be a teapot was a teapot. Nothing more and nothing less. Just teapots. But I was up and beyond in Dublin last week, baby-sitting little Kieran, his mammy and daddy away in London for an advertising conference. So, anyway, I took him for a walk down by the canal—the water's filthy these days, floating with Styrofoam cups, all that smog and neon along the banks, even a couple of condoms, floating on the water. I kid you not! Who would use those things anyway, Moira? Like your Sean says, it must be like washing your feet with your socks on! But, like I was saying, we were throwing some bread to the ducks, and all of a sudden little Kieran says to me, he says: "Look at those teapots over there, Granny." And him pointing to a couple of boys wrapped together like slices of bread underneath the Leeson Street Bridge, kissing in broad daylight. Teapots. I ask you, Moira. Apparently something to do with the way the spout curves.

We'll give that cleanser a moment to settle now, Moira, then we'll get started with the foundation. Sad to say, anyway, Larry and Paula look like they're emigrating too. Paula got offered a job with that crowd, Saatchi and Saatchi. They're going to enroll little Kieran in some private school on the outskirts of London. There's another one will grow up with an English accent. Dropping h's all over the place. A terrible shame. And

he'll see more than his fair share of teapots over there, I'll tell
you. That sort of thing goes on all the time in London. It's as
bad as Amsterdam. Before you know it there'll be none of us
McAllisters left in Ireland at all. Sure, don't you remember the
time we almost went ourselves? 1947, wasn't it? Anniversary of
D-Day, if I'm not mistaken.

Don't you remember us walking down the main street and
those two Yankee soldiers sauntering by O'Connor's butcher
shop with the big red awning? Decked out in the full regalia,
handsome as Sunday. Recovering from the war, of course. The
lads in town didn't like them at all. Overpaid, oversexed, and
over here. A wee bit of jealousy, I'd say, because aren't those
Americans awful good-looking people? Great teeth and all.
Anyway. Remember? You in your ochre blouse and your linen
skirt and me myself in my favorite green cardigan, the one with
the flowers crocheted on the side. Both of us after making our
faces up lovely. And up come the two Yankee boys, asking us
what was it a fella could do of an evening in a town like this?
And, before you know it, we're out there driving down the
Cork road with the windows open and them singing all sorts of
curious songs. *Heidy-deighty, Christ Almighty, who the hell are we?*
Wham bam thank you ma'am we're the infantry! And us covering
our ears, pretending like we were shocked. Out into the coun-
tryside, under those huge stars, and them saying that the car was
broken down so they could walk us back to town in the dark.
Talk about conniving. And us pretending like we were scared,
so we could lean into them. A summer night, wasn't it?

But we were tempted. Let it be said, here and now, we were

117

tempted. Now, of course, my Eoin and your Sean wouldn't need to hear that, but we were tempted to be sure. Oh yes. On we go now, anyway. A bit of foundation. Just a dab here. I brought my finest, of course. We'll just get in there under your chin a little bit. Skim off the surplus here now, with my old camel's hair brush. You're looking really great now. Ah, it's a sad world sometimes, but it gives you such funny stories.

Who knows, but we could have been married to some Yanks! Funny thing that, when you think about it. At least for you it was love at first sight with Sean, and isn't that what makes the world go around? *Love and marriage, love and marriage, go together like a horse and carriage, ladeedadeedada, ladeedadeedadee, you can't have one without the other.* Me oh my. Can hardly remember the words now. Between yourself and myself and the walls, sometimes I almost regret putting the cart before the horse, so to speak, marrying Eoin like I did. He was never exactly—well, he was a quiet man. But, well, damn it all anyway, there's enough badmouthing done in this world without me adding to it. Isn't that right? Too many bickerers and begrudgers all over the place. My Eoin gave me a good home, God bless his soul, treated me right, even if now and then I got a little uppity with him. Enough said now. He was always very fond of you as well Moira. Always said nice things about you. Loved your pot roast, and I'm not just saying that. He was heard to say, more than once, that he'd run to Dublin and back if he knew one of your pot roasts was waiting for him.

And talking of men who are quick on their feet now, Moira! That time you met your Sean. That was so funny, wasn't it? At that dance in Greenore, you wearing that red velvet dress just a little bit off the shoulder. Daring for the times. 1951. October, if I'm not mistaken. Or was it November? Getting a bit on the cold side, if I remember correctly, and you wouldn't wear a cardigan over your dress. Partial to showing off, you were, and why not? You have a body on you that the rest of us have always envied, that's for sure. Anyway, remember that night? That drafty old hall with the grimy windows? Us sitting there, me with my Eoin, newly married and cuddling, and you beside us, the gooseberry just waiting for a man. Indeed you were! Don't be codding me now. Hackling for a man you were. But you were beautiful that night. You were too. With the red dress, face all done, and those fancy new stockings. And up he comes, your Sean, skipping over the floor, from the other side of the hall, his hat sideways, smelling of Brylcreem, that chip in his teeth showing, over to you, saying, "Excuse me, any chance of a dance before I get carpet burns on me tongue?" I almost wet myself laughing! Carpet burns on his tongue! And then both of you out there, dancing and laughing. You always said it was love at first sight, and why not? He's the nicest man. Him always talking you up a storm. Anyway, here I am, rambling away as usual. He gave me your note today, your Sean did. Said to me: "Do her face up good now, Eileen. It's a big journey."

And a big journey it is too. The foundation now, Moira, is on like a dream. Trust me. And, as you say, you want to be traveling like a princess. And that you will be. We got so handy with the makeup, didn't we? Even when the kids were born, and the beauty parlor was shut down, we'd always find some time for it. Trying out the lemon to get rid of the freckles. And those oatmeal face packs, Lord, they were great!

But, and let me say it, here and now, I'll never ever ever forget the time you messed up my hair. I was a crotchety old bear for months afterward, and I'm sorry for it. But you have to think about it in the light of the time. Not two months after Matthew was born. You saying I'd look great if I got a bit of the stray gray out of the hair. Pushing the auburn look. Auburn this. Auburn that. Auburn the other thing. My head was down there in the sink in your bungalow saying, "Moira, are you sure about this?" "Sure, I'm sure," you said. Not a bother on you. And for five weeks afterward my head was a fluorescent orange. Like a nuclear carrot, I was! Luminous! A tourist attraction! Everyone thought it very funny when July twelfth rolled around. All of them saying: "Oh, we can send Eileen up to Belfast for Orangeman's Day."

I was fuming, and I'm really sorry about what I did with your sunflowers. I know I never told you. But it was me. I'm very sorry. Lopped their heads off with a scissors, I was so mad. But the hair was really awful, you must admit. Come off it now! It was! Don't be fooling me. Eoin wouldn't touch me for weeks. Not that he was a mad passionate man anyway. He kept calling me a left footer. The kids all thought I'd gone barmy. Me, having to wear that awful scarf, the one with the pictures of the pound notes on it, all around town for God knows how long. Rinsing my hair every day, trying to get the dye out. But, that's said and done, and we can laugh about it now.

But we were pretty handy all the same, weren't we? Even

when it was rationed, we could always find some. Sure, remember when we got those red stones that when you licked them, they'd give off a bit of paint? Down by the river when we were kids. And using the sugar water to keep the hair up. And the berry juice we'd smear on our cheeks when we had nothing else. The fun we had with those. Speaking of, Moira, here we go with the rouge now. Yardley. That rose perle tint you've always been fond of.

Strange that. Never really thought of it that way. Those stones we'd find, down by the river, us little girls, in exactly the same place where your Sean and young Liam wanted to build your bungalow. Moira, those lettuce-and-tomato sandwiches! Those flasks of tea! Weren't those the times? Your Liam there working on the house. Up we'd go with his lunch and he'd say, him hanging out of the rafters: "Mam, Auntie Eileen, are you sure yez put enough salad cream on these things today?" Always mad keen on the lettuce and tomato. And then us down to the town with another flask and a few brown bags for the men. Us meeting in the park and spreading out the big white tablecloth. Your Sean forever leaving all those dirty thumbprints on the tablecloth. Terrible. And don't you remember the day I took the driving test! Sean leaving that dirty great spanner in the middle of the passenger seat by mistake. Me so nervous that I forgot about it and along comes the driving inspector and sits on the damn thing. Moira, it must be said that he was a bit of a poofter, wearing those cream pants, don't you think? Him so snotty and dignified and stupid that he didn't say a thing. Him failing me and all. And me not even hitting the curb on the three-point turn. Livid, I was. But it was worth the price of admission, that was. That big slobber of oil on his arse pants. Him waddling off. A teapot, as your Kieran would say.

This rouge is fabulous stuff. Blending in wonderfully. Amazing what they can do nowadays. Listen to me ramble and me making a mess with the makeup! God! Your sunflowers. I'm still thinking about your sunflowers. And the way you were going to enter them in the flower competition. Sorry now. I really am. Along I came and snippety-snip, they were gone.

Well, it'll be family now, the next few days, us all back together again. The children never understand at times like these, and it's just as well that they have a bit of fun. We'll get little Orla and Fiona and Michelle and we'll teach them how to put on some makeup. Maybe even see if some of the young girls at the beauty parlor will allow me to take up a chair and teach the kids some tricks of the trade. Oh me, oh my, wouldn't that be a racket! We'll take the boys and bring them down to the bridge, lash together some fishing poles and maybe even go for a plunge, what with the hot weather we've been having. Give the rest of us time. All of us adults together. I know I said some bad things about my Eoin, but I really wish he was here. But. Well! I'm happy enough. I really am. The letters from the kids and all, keeping up the house, and baking the odd bit of bread. Up to Dublin occasionally to baby-sit. And just walking about the town. The river's bad, though, as you know. That chemical factory has been sending men down here with all their Geiger counters or whatever it is they call them. Soon we'll all be walking around glowing. Another go-around with the orange hair for me, I suppose. Just a little extra rouge here. Don't be worrying. Moira, you have the most gorgeous cheekbones! I've always envied those cheekbones.

Now let me just have a minute here now and we'll start on the eyes. A dab with the pencil first, I think. The moss-colored one. Up above the lashes here. Ah-ha. Anyway. Umm. Just a touch here. Isn't it terrible, though? There they were, promising a hundred jobs and all we get is a river we can hardly swim in anymore. But, my God, I was down there the other day and you should see some of the bathing suits the young girls are wearing! Little thongs thin as twigs. Pieces of cloth no thicker than thread. Down there flossing, Moira! I ask you. Leaving not a thing to the imagination. But why not? When you have it, flaunt it, I suppose. To hell with God and country. Now, I don't really mean that, Moira, but you know what I mean. It's not as if we were the purest things since snow or sliced bread. I mean, we were given to a bit of wiggling too, weren't we, when we had it? Not that we ever wore swimsuits like that. Let me stand back a minute and size you up.

A sight for sore eyes, you are. What do you think? Some more? All right so. Here we go. Marvelous. Jiminy cricket, but you're looking great. Then we'll see what we can do with the eye shadow and the mascara. We'll give you that green, a bit of light color under the eyebrows. Those eyes of yours always so green. Ah, Moira. You made me happy with that note of yours, strange as it may seem. Your Sean woke up this morning and the first thing he did was he phoned me, told me the news, saying that he had this envelope that he had tucked away for years in the bottom drawer of his dresser. Drove over to the house and handed it to me. Both of us crying. No airs about you. There's never been an air about you. That's how I'd like to do it myself. No fuss or bother.

It was a lovely note all the same. Such a lovely idea. When in the world did you write it? Sean said he had it for years and that many's the time he wanted to open it. Anyway, we went down to McCartan's in the rain to arrange the arrangements, and old man McCartan saying: "That's a very strange request, I'm not sure if we can do it." And your Sean—he loves you so much, he really does—taking him aside and saying that he'd give Mc-Cartan a few extra bob if he'd let me do your face. McCartan's a bit of a rat for the money sometimes. Hemmed and hawed for a moment. Sean slipped him another fiver and McCartan got everything ready for me—fixed you up in a way of peace and all. But him still trying to tell me that it might overwhelm me. Overwhelm me! I ask you! After all the times I've done this self-same thing. Go away out of that, Mister McCartan, I said to him. There's nobody better for the job. I'll do her up right. Sure we'll have a little natter and we'll talk about old times.

Liam's huge bicycle with the purple mudguards! Orla winning the footrace at the County Fair! You burning the pot roast the day Haughey resigned! The holiday in Bray, and Eoin walking the promenade and his hat blowing off and the seagull leaving a dollop on his head! Me oh my. Haven't we had the life of it? And the things we remember! Him ranting and raving and effing and blinding all over the place, what with that seagull stuff all over his handkerchief! Moira, I could talk all night, but look at me here, and I still haven't finished your eyes, not to mention the lipstick and everyone due to see you shortly. I better get cracking.

Seems like half the town went to the airport today to pick up people flying in. Shannon and Dublin. They'll be in later today to say hello. Even young Fiachra. Him and his tulips from Amsterdam. What a scoundrel he is. Okay, now, this color is just perfect. Coal green fading out gently. Perfect. It really is. Makes you look like a million dollars. You recall Fiachra, and him hardly having a hair on his head until he was three years old? Just never grew, did it? You taking him down to the supermarket on Main Street when Ciara was down sick with the flu in seventy-six. And that old bat, Mrs. Roche, coming up to you and asking why in the world you'd allow your grandson to have all his hair shaved off. And then her whispering in your ear: "Was it your sister Eileen who gave him that awful haircut?" And you smacking her in the jaw with a cauliflower for the implication! Ah Lord, how I would have loved to have been a fly on the wall. Serves her right. Anyway, I know it's rude to whisper, but did you know that her youngest is up the pole, as they say? True as God, Moira. Six months gone. What do you make of that?

Here we go, and we'll get the extra smudge off the eyelashes. We'll be done awful soon. Just let me get the lipstick absolutely right. That's the most important thing, I always say. Get the lips right and you've the battle won. Launch a thousand ships, you will. Here we go. Yes. Ah-ha. Pencil first, of course. You and Sean at your wedding, that's the funniest photograph. Him standing outside the church, all that confetti over his shoulders, a smile on him to beat the band, the lily in his breast pocket, all the people milling around and right there—smack dab in the middle of his cheek—that huge lipstick mark. Spent half the morning getting the lipstick just right and then you went and smeared it all over his cheek. Lord, woman! Those were the days! Listen to me ramble, and a hundred people waiting to see you. Mrs. Burden made the sandwiches and Tommy Farrell got a ton of whiskey for the evening, Father Colligan's the one to say mass, and Miss Bennet, from the school, is putting together some lovely flowers. This lipstick is really something special, let me tell you, makes your lips full and really compliments you. Estée Lauder, if you don't mind! Pale rose.

Talking like a runaway train, I am. Ah, but you were never able to get a word in edgewise, were you, Moira? Always me rattling away, no matter what. From day one on. And, sure, I'll visit you every week. Sean has got a lovely quiet spot, not too far from where your young Liam is. The only thing is that the old factory's going to belch up the odd bit of smoke in your way, otherwise you'd probably have a clear vision almost all the way to Dublin. A few yards away from that huge old chestnut tree you'll be. And never lonely, what with the boys out gathering conkers and me, myself, I'll come out there and run my mouth off as usual. Yes indeed. Now, I better get a grip of myself, because I promised myself I wasn't going to cry. And you know when I make a promise to myself. But I'll tell you, and here's another promise now.

You know what I'm going to do next week? Here's what I'm

going to do. I'm going to buy a packet of sunflower seeds. That's what I'm going to do. To hell with everything else. Down in McKenna's. Going to go to McKenna's, buy myself a little trowel and some fertilizer. That's what I'm going to do. Wear my old clogs and my big hat. Walk out to the chestnut tree. Plant the seeds, away from the shade. Then sit back and watch them grow. Every day. And if anybody comes along with a snippety-snip, I'll knock them arse-over-backwards into the middle of next week. And that's a promise. From me to you. Water them every day. Now let me just take a step back here and have a look at you. Just going to step back. Water them every day. Ah-ha. Just going to stand here. Just a moment now. That's what I'm going to do.

Moira, let me tell you something. Let me tell you. You look smashing. You really do. You really, really do. Absolutely smashing. A lovely peaceful smile on you. My God, you look smashing. Really, really smashing.

FROM MANY, ONE

I used to love the way she painted quarters. There were many fabulous colors that she could concoct on them. Don't ask me how she got them to stick, because she had big stubby fingers for a little woman, and she must have used a very small paintbrush. But I'd come home from work in the evenings around five or six and she'd be in the back greenhouse, which we had turned into a little studio, and she'd be bent over the table, just all caught up in making these coins look colorful. She never really let me come into the studio. That was her space. There were times that I'd watch her from the kitchen and she would just billow around in her big white apron, past all the flowerpots, like she was being blown around by that big fan. Dallas is hot anyway in the summer, but this was so hot you could fry eggs in there.

I never saw the quarters until one Saturday afternoon when she was out canoeing the Brazos with Jeanie. I was trying to fix her old Karmen Ghia, looking for a screwdriver so I could take the clips off the distributor cap. They were rusted on. So I went into the greenhouse, where I reckoned there were some extra tools, and all these coins were out lying on the table. There were rows and rows of them, all painted.

The eagle sometimes had these weird multi-colored wings. Sometimes there was a small picture—a television, a radio tower, a car—on the eagle's chest. The olive branch was always yellow for some reason. The strangest ones were when you could see into George Washington's cranium. I mean, here's this guy that everyone goes nuts about, father of the country and all that, then all of a sudden he's got a tiny picture of an apple in his brainbox, or weird animals on that big curl of hair at the back, or he's wearing lipstick, or that little tail down the back of his wig looks like a map of Central America. Then there was always these little dots along the year. 1974 had yellow dots, 1989 had green ones, that sort of weird stuff. Then, in all the spaces, there were these psychedelic colours. She colored in the writing, and one of them said, in bright pink, IN O WE TRUST, where she didn't color in the G or the D.

I've never been much into modern art or anything. I mean, I like Remington and stuff, but not that other crap. But this wasn't crap, see. This was kind of funny, really. I liked them.

Laura wasn't pleased when she found out that I'd been in there. "That's my studio, for crissake." She said the *my* real loud.

"It's my house," I said.

"It's my work."

"You're my wife."

"And you're my goddamn husband."

130

We'd been married for three years, and it was around Valentine's Day, but we'd both forgotten. Maybe it was all the work I was doing in the labs—I was a lab assistant to a professor who was building phylogenetic trees of sparrows, breaking down their DNA and grouping them—sometimes ten, twelve hours a day. She liked to draw all the time. She was from a good family, her father was an investment banker in Houston, and I guess she spent a lot of her teenage years doing paintings.

Once I woke up and caught her sitting beside the bed, drawing my face on one of these quarters. She was hunched over the bed with these tiny paintbrushes and a palette, her hair tied back, a real serious look on her face. Boy, did I ever want to see that one. But I looked and looked in the greenhouse, and I never found it. I knew it was around somewhere, because she told me she never spent them. I searched for hours, under the table, in all the plant pots, down under the wrought-iron stand, on the ledges, but it never showed up. I expect maybe she painted me with big black eyes, my hair receding, big jowls and all that sort of thing, even though that's not true.

But I did find some other coins. They were self-portraits, her face painted on top of Washington's, big long mane of red hair running down her back, that one eye all painted with mascara, her lips flaring out. She was pretty, all right. I could see why she did it. She'd always been pretty, right from the day I met her. So, I took one of those quarters and put it in my wallet. I kind of liked to look at it when I was at work. Most of my job was extracting the blood samples.

I came home from work one night and she wasn't there, so I

went on down to the bar. We live in a fairly good neighborhood and the nearest bar is down by the highway. It's a dark
bar, lots of people hanging out in the corners. You see some
strange ones there. But the thing about it is, it's amazing the
things you don't know about people. I was sitting there at the
bar, talking with the bartender, Paul, and it turns out this guy
does computers on the side. There's nobody there hardly, so
we talk for a long time, about computer sequencing, research,
and things about sparrows and stuff, when all of a sudden he
points down at my hand and laughs, then sort of grabs my
cheek.

"Doing a little on the side?" he says to me. I look down and
realize that I've been fingering this quarter in my hands for the
last half hour. It's the portrait of Laura. That face is full of
yellows and reds.

I ask him what he's talking about, and he reaches in under
the counter and pulls out about twenty of these quarters. They
spill through his goddamn fingers. Jefferson with a peace sign
on his forehead, another with the LIBERTY shortened to BERT,
the eagle wearing a bra, all sorts of colors everywhere. Says he
likes to collect them himself when customers come from the
Rose down the street. Says to me that the guys at the Rose, and
sometimes the girls, bring the quarters in. One of the afternoon
strippers there makes them.

"They put them in the jukebox," he says, "so at the end of
the night they know which quarters are theirs. You see red ones
and green ones and blue ones and all sorts. But these are great.
This chick is an artist. I'd like to see this chick dance."

I don't know much about things, but I do know that it's amazing, the things we don't know. I went home that evening and wanted to drive that Karmen Ghia right through the greenhouse, plow it right on through, shatter it into pieces. Laura got home, late, and just went straight on out to the greenhouse. She looked awful young and pretty. She swept past me and said: "You look tired, honey." She actually said that. She said "honey." I sat there, in the kitchen, wondering what sort of face she was drawing this time.

FISHING THE

SLOE-BLACK RIVER

The women fished for their sons in the sloe-black river that ran through the small Westmeath town, while the fathers played football without their sons, in a field half a mile away. Low shouts drifted like lazy swallows over the river, interrupting the silence of the women. They were casting with ferocious hope, twenty-six of them in unison, in a straight line along the muddy side of the low-slung river wall, whipping the rods back over their shoulders. They had pieces of fresh bread mashed onto hooks so that when they cast their lines, the bread volleyed out over the river and hung for a moment, making curious contours in the air—cartwheels and tumbles and plunges. The bread landed with a soft splash on the water, and the ripples met each other gently.

The aurora borealis was beginning to finger the sky with light the color of skin, wine bottles, and the amber of the town's football jerseys. Drowsy clouds drifted, catching the colors from the north. A collie dog slept in the doorway of the only pub. The main street tumbled with litter.

The women along the wall stood yards apart, giving each other room so their lines wouldn't tangle. Mrs. Conheeny wore a headscarf patterned with Corgi dogs, the little animals yelping at the side of her ashy hair. She had tiny dollops of dough still stuck under her fingernails. There were splashes of mud on her Wellingtons. She bent her back into the familiar work of reeling in the empty line. Each time she cast, she curled her upper lip, scrunching up the crevices around her cheeks. She was wondering how Father Marsh, the old priest for whom she did housekeeping, was doing as goalkeeper. The joke around town was that he was only good for saving souls. As she spun a little line out from the reel she worried that her husband, at right-halfback, might be feeling the ache in his knee from ligaments torn long ago.

Leaning up against the river wall, tall and bosom-burdened, she sighed and whisked her fishing rod through the air.

Beside her Mrs. Harrington, the artist's wife, was a salmon leap of energy, thrashing the line back and forth as deftly as a fly-fisherwoman, ripping crusts from her own loaves, impaling them on the big gray hook and spinning them out over the water's blackness, frantically tapping her feet up and down on the muddy bank. Mrs. Harrington's husband had been shoved in at left full-forward in the hope that he might poke a stray shot away in a goalmouth frenzy. But by all accounts—or so Mr. Conheeny said—the watercolor man wasn't worth a barman's fart on the football field. Then again, they all laughed, at least he was a warm body. He could fill a position against the other teams in the county, all of whom still managed to gallop, here and there, with young bones.

Mrs. Conheeny scratched at her forehead. Not a bite, not a bit, not a brat around, she thought as she reeled in her line and watched a blue chocolate wrapper get caught in a gust of wind, then float down onto the water.

The collie left the door of the pub, ambling down along the main street, past the row of townhouses, nosing in the litter outside the newsagents. Heavy roars keened through the air as the evening stole shapes. Each time the women heard the whistle blow, they raised their heads in the hope that the match was finished so they could unsnap the rods and bend toward home with their picnic baskets.

Mrs. Conheeny watched Mrs. Hynes across the river, her face plastered with makeup, tentatively clawing at a reel. Mrs. King was there with her graphite rod. Mrs. McDaid had come up with the idea of putting currants in her bread. Mrs. O'Shaughnessy was whipping away with a long slender piece of bamboo—did she think she was fishing in the Mississippi? Mrs. Bergen, her face scrunched in pain from the arthritis, was hoping her fingers might move a little better, like they used to on the antique accordion. Mrs. Kelly was sipping from her little silver flask of the finest Jameson's. Mrs. Hogan was casting with firefly flicks of the wrist. Mrs. Docherty was hauling in her line, as if gathering folds in her dress. And Mrs. Hennessy was gently peeling the crust from a slice of Brennan's.

Farther down along the pebbledashed wall, Mrs. McCarton

was gently humming a bit of a song. *Flow on lovely river flow gently along, by your waters so clear sounds the lark's merry song.* Her husband captained the team, a barrel of a man who, when he was young, consistently scored a hat trick. But the team hadn't won a game in two years, ever since the children had begun their drift.

They waited, the women, and they cast, all of them together.

When the long whistle finally cut through the air and the colors took on forms that flung themselves against the northern sky, the women slowly unsnapped their rods and placed the hooks in the lowest eyes. They looked at each other and nodded sadly. Another useless day fishing. Opening picnic baskets and lunch boxes, they put the bread away and waited for the line of Ford Cortinas and Vauxhalls and Opel Kaddets and Mr. Hogan's blue tractor to trundle down and pick them up.

Their husbands arrived with their amber jerseys splattered with mud, their faces long in another defeat, cursing under taggles of pipes, their old bones creaking at the joints.

Mrs. Conheeny readjusted her scarf and watched for her husband's car. She saw him lean over and ritually open the door even before he stopped. She ducked her head to get in, put the rod and basket in the backseat. She waved to the women who were still waiting, then took off her headscarf.

"Any luck, love?" he asked.

She shook her head: "I didn't even get a bite."

She looked out to the sloe-black river as they drove off, then sighed. One day she would tell him how useless it all was, this fishing for sons, when the river looked not a bit like the

Thames or the Darling or the Hudson or the Loire or even the Rhine itself, where their own three sons were working in a car factory. He slapped his hands on the steering wheel and said with a sad laugh: "Well, fuck it anyway, we really need some new blood in midfield," although she knew that he too would go fishing that night, silently slipping out, down to the river, to cast in vain.

AROUND THE BEND

AND BACK AGAIN

S trange bloody cuckoo, that one. Couple of rhododendrons hanging in her hair. Chewing on her fingernails
like she's starving. Spent yesterday afternoon circling one of the
puddles out by the greenhouse, just walking round and round
like there's no tomorrow. Trailed mud all over the bloody floor
after I swishbuckled the fucking thing to a shine. Nothing to be
said for consideration. But she's not half bad all the same.
Dressing gown giving a bit of a peep there, right down to
the brown of the nipple. The way she just stares there out the
window, you'd swear there was something on television in the
bloody stars. Here we go with the Plough and the Stars, star-
ring Tom bloody Cruise. She needs a bit of a haircut though,
those long strands going mad all the way over her mouth.
Dolores, giving her a bath yesterday, said she was a bit ripe
under the armpits. Who wouldn't be after hanging around
town for days without a bloody bath? Singing some fucking

song when they stuck a toothbrush down her gob. And enough tranquilizers in her to knock out a good horse.

She's your one from the railway family. Recognized her the minute they dragged her in. Moved here from Dublin with her Ma and Da about twelve years back and lived up there in that old orange caboose at the bottom of the hills. Strange fucking place that, railway carriage sitting out in the middle of nowhere. Propped up on cement blocks and all. Surrounded by flower beds and stone walls and green fields, no wonder she went barmy. Choo fucking choo here we go down the valley. She was choo-chooing all right when the cops brought her up here, smashing her little brown curls against the door of the squad car, going crazy with something about her caboose.

Never forget my first sight of that thing years back, on the back of a huge bloody truck, getting carted up from the railway station. Along it comes down main street, almost shit myself. Big orange thing, gone a bit rusty after sitting at the ends of the tracks for so long. One hell of a job that. Must have cost a damn fortune for her old man to hire that truck and a winch and ten hefty men to help cart it up to the hills. I remember her looking out the window as it went round the corner, bewildered as fuck, her no more than eight years old, ribbons in her hair. I was only six myself, that big old bandage on my hand from when I let a firework go off in my fist. Along I went running after the damn thing but it was way too fast. All the other lads went up to the valley later on, where they were propping it up on blocks and asked if she could come out to play. *No,* says her Da, *she has to study.* We all knew he was a weirdo after that.

Her Da was one of those fellas who look at the stars and make maps. Like Darryl Hannah in that film *Roxanne* with your man with the big nose. But her Da was just a little fella in a black beret. Always hanging out at that caboose he was. There was a huge bloody telescope sticking out of the roof sometimes. Talk was that he slept during the day and worked at night and once he even made a trip to California to look through a mighty telescope there. Might make an accounting for the Plough and the Stars stuff that she's up to tonight, rocking away there by the window, kneeling on the bed, staring out the window like she's saying her prayers. Right beside Maggie the Moaner too. That's some pair. And just wait until Georgie girl comes back. There'll be ructions then, I swear.

Her Ma was a strange one too. Wrote books on flower arranging. Grand topic that, as long as you've had a decent lobotomy in the last six months. She was always off to the flower shows with all sorts of buckets in the backseat of the car. How she kept from bouncing around with all the fucking potholes in the road around here I'll never know. Used to see her the odd time down by the river examining flowers with one of those microscope things. There's some strange people live around here, that's for sure.

I was having a nap in the stock room and the nurses were nattering away about her. Seems her old man liked the horses as well as the stars. Before the car crash on the Swinford Road he put a load of money on some horse called Tycho in the fifth at Leopardstown. Old Tycho fell at the second fence and the old man never told anyone that the caboose suddenly belonged to some bank up beyond in Dublin. Rough that. One day you're doing grand, living in a caboose, the old fella looking at the stars, the old dear tending the flowerpots and things are not so bad at all at all. The next day your Ma and Da are smashed in a car on that fucking bend in the Swinford Road, the will is worth shit, and before you know it the bank owns the caboose and you haven't two pennies to rub together. Bob's your uncle, you're out on the street, two plastic bags in your hands, Dunnes Stores better value beats them all.

No wonder she's sitting there shaking like crazy.

Nurses were saying that the bank let her live in the caboose for the best part of six months after the crash, and that's true enough because I saw her up there one day myself, and she was just sitting in a lawn chair watching the world go by, happy as Larry. Gave her a wave but I don't think she saw me. But the bank is doing talks with the mining company now, so she's out on her ear, poor girl. Bank manager gave her a loan of a flat down by the newspaper offices a few days ago, but she wouldn't stay. Bit stupid that. Guards found her walking up the road towards the caboose every bloody minute of the day, her screaming and shouting something about looking after her old dear's flower beds. I seen her myself once down under the bridge and she was roaring her head off, all those flowers in her hair. Gave her a wave then too, but it was the same bloody

144

thing. That's madness if you ask me. Standing freezing in the middle of the bloody river.

And she's a wild one too. Had to grab a hold of her feet when they brought her here. Strong as an ox. Wonder Woman, how are ya. Barney was a bit rough with her all the same. He shouldn't have slapped her across the gob like that when the nurses weren't looking. Said she spat at him, but Barney's a fierce one for lying sometimes. *Bet she's another one for breaking the toilet seats wait till you see,* that's what Barney said. He's probably right but he shouldn't have slapped her one anyway. Barney-boy has a thing with the toilet seats. Hates scrubbing the damn things. He's always bulling about the globs of shite left around the bowl. And he gets even worse when the madwomen get to standing on the seat and aiming from on high.

Still and all, she's quiet now after all the rumpus. Strange what might go on in a head like that, her there staring out the window of the dorm. Dolores said she caught a goo of her many a time up there on the roof of the caboose with her old man, before the crash. Staring at these maps with a small red torch they were. Something to do with night vision or something. Help them watch the goings on. There'll be none of that for a while. Only stars she'll be seeing are the ones from those little yellow pills they're shoving down her throat. Her and Georgina'll have a ball when they bring Georgie back from Dublin. That's what Georgina gets for being a speed freak anyway. Ice water injected into the veins. Nasty stuff. Sends the heart rate rocketing. Her and Georgie'll be the youngest ones in the whole bloody ward. And Georgie's a fierce one for pissing on the floors. In I go to clean the toilet up and it's slippery as all fuck.

Johnnie Logan's going nuts over the mining boys. Says they should stay the hell out. But he's all set, he is, with his Opel bloody Manta and his four-bedroom house and a seat on the County Council. Man like that doesn't need a new job, unlike me and Barney. If he keeps those mining boys out it'll be a good thump in the head from Barney, that's for sure. And I'll never vote for the bastard again. He used to be one hell of a boyo, getting that strike settled for the union and all, but like Barney says he's barking up the wrong tree this time.

Ferocious bloody hangover this evening. Out on the piss in the Humbert with Barney in the broads of broad daylight. Smithwick's. *Nectar of the dogs,* says Barney. And a fierce drink for the scuts.

Anyway, it's all signed sealed and delivered, says Barney. The bank sold your woman's caboose to the mining company. Off they are now doing speculations in the hills. There's gold in dem dere hills, as the boys in the wild west say. Word around is that there might be jobs when the mining boys get their act together, which'd be a damnsight better than cleaning the bin, that's for sure. Johnnie Logan's bulling, but it serves him right, him and all the other greenies around. There'll be a road up the mountain, no ifs, ands, or buts. They can all go to Kerry or Majorca or the south of bloody France if they want a bit of peace and quiet.

Went up there myself for a goo. Mining boys already put a big insignia on the side of the caboose. Picture of a mountain with the sun coming up over it. It'll be a sunny bloody morning if they hire myself and Barney, that's for sure. Those boys have money. You can be sure of that. We'll be laughing and it might even bring a few of the lads home from Amsterdam or the Bronx or wherever the hell they're gone. They put some barbed wire around the old carriage and already got themselves a few JCBs and a couple of churners, a pile of gravel and a big blue Dumpster. There's no flower beds there any more, that's for sure. Looks a bit different than it used to but that's the way it goes. Jobs are jobs. There'll be hell to pay if they don't hire local lads, all the same.

Your woman must know about the caboose because she threw a nasty one tonight. Out they were doing all sorts of maneuvers to hold her down, the Heimlich and all that stuff. The only doctor on was that skinny bloke who stinks of garlic. Nurses had to call me out from the kitchen, where I was doing the scrubbing, to give them a hand. Six of us there including Barney, but he went a bit easier with her this evening. Dressing gown all over the place and she's a good-looking woman, all the same. Barney asked me if I sprung a hard-on. He's a filthy bastard sometimes. Anyway, out of her pockets comes tumbling a load of sachets of sugar that she must have stolen from the bowls in the dining area. Dozens of the damn things spilling all over the floor. In the little white packets. Maybe she has a sweet tooth.

Eventually calmed the hissy-fit though, the lot of us together. On with the gray gown, out with the shoelaces, give us that necklace, darling, and it's off down to solitary with the soft white stuff on the walls. Don't be banging your little brown curls around this time.

Must be awful hard all the same, losing the parents and the caboose like that. The nurses call her Ofeelia on account of the flowers in her hair. Can't help feeling a bit sorry for her, even if Barney says it's her own fault. Twenty years old and it's not much better than the fucking slophouse.

Still no sign of the Georgie one. They must be doing all sorts of tests on her up beyond in the big smoke. Dymphna O'Connor got the thumbs up today and it's off back to Kiltimagh for her. But the place was a fucking mess. There was a tampon shoved down the inside of the third stall and the rubber gloves had taken a hike. Mary Marshall at it again. They should teach that woman some manners. Barney told me a funny joke about Eve in the river but I can't for the life of me remember it now. One of these days me and Barney are going to get new jobs. No doubt about it. We'll be up there with the mining boys wearing three-piece suits and colorful ties and the doctors at the bin can lick the piss off the floors themselves.

Ofeelia was very quiet in solitary today. Often wondered why I never saw more of her around town, her being a fine thing and all. By all accounts, so say the nurses, her Da had a fierce battle with the board of education to keep her at home. Just imagine that. Didn't even have a debs dance or anything. A bit like myself I suppose, since I only did the Inter and didn't get a chance to dance with the old dickie bow on. Living in that caboose she probably never even had a chance to see any new films either. Christ. That's not living.

The nurses were saying that her Da taught her the weirdest bloody stuff, him always up in arms about chemicals in the air and the peat bogs and all that other stuff they talk about. He was a friend of Logan's and the greenies. Seems to me you have to be pretty bloody rich before you start talking about all that stuff. You can see them there on the TV, protesting the whales and the dolphins and all. There's some graffiti in the women's toilet that says NUKE THE GAY WHALES, which is pretty damn funny when you think about it.

She has the greenest eyes I ever saw. I'll say that much for her. And quoting some strange bloody poetry too when she's down there in solitary. All about these turtles and stuff. Doctor Garlic went to take her out today but she threw another nasty one. It was back into the white room for her, a shove in the back from Doctor G. That fella's a screamer if ever I saw one. He shouldn't be treating the patients like that, that's all I have to say.

She's a headcase, that one. Acting nice as could be for the last two days and back in the dorm, she is. Slopping out the stalls and who rolls in but herself. Oops, I say, it's closed for a minute or two. Down she leans and, straight in the eyes, asks me if I could buy her a few bottles of syrup down at the shops, then slips me a fiver. Can I trust ya? she says, sounding normal as could be, even though they slapped a few of the yellow boys down her gob earlier on. Dressing gown hanging down awful low again. Barney would have had it right, but I never told him. Up she stands, with a bit of a wink and down the corridor until Dolores finds her and guides her back to the dorm by the elbow, awful gentle like.

So I bought the syrup, why not. Cost me an extra eighty-six pence. Went in, when they were all at dinner, and slipped the bottles under her bed. Didn't say a word to Barney. He'd be slagging me something fierce. Took to calling me Hamlet for some reason when I said she wasn't half-bad-looking. That bastard is always in the storeroom pulling his plum anyway.

There I was, doing a number on the corridors at about four in the morning, and the night nurses must have been sleeping or else she's quiet as a fucking mouse. *You're a savior,* she says to me, and slips four pink flowers across the floor. Syrup all over the front of her dressing gown. The flowers got a bit wet on account of the mop water, but I dried them out in the flat later on and put them in a jar. Anyway, I've a funny feeling she's not half-mad at all. Asked me did I know where the caboose was. I said yeah, course I do. Then before she went waltzing back down the corridor she asked me to take some photos of the bloody thing for her. To hang above her bed because she's homesick. Christ.

At the bloody sugar she was again tonight. And splatters of syrup all over her dressing gown. Georgie's back, awful quiet, and she isn't talking to a soul.

Those mining boys have the life of it up there. Two BMWs down by the gate. Barney says that the only difference between a cactus and a Beemer is that one has the pricks on the outside. He's a funny bastard sometimes. But I wouldn't say no if they put one out the front door for me, that's for sure. Dublin license plates on them. Sitting outside the caboose, shiny as could be. They hired McLaverty and three of his fucking crew to make the tarmacadam road up from the main one, over the hills and down into the valley there. It's a job all right, but it's not mine. Still and all McLaverty said they'll be hiring if things prove to be going all right.

There's ructions in the Council. Johnnie Logan even said the hills are holy and they should take their mining company back to Ballyfermot and dig up a few horse bones for the knackers up there. That fella has a mouth on him for a politician. Still and all there's no job like a job that pays, that's what I say.

Got to thinking about old Ofeelia when I was up there snapping away. Bloody photos'd break her heart, even if she is a touch on the mad side. No flowers or anything. Anyway this security bloke comes out and asks me if I'm from the newspaper, then tells me not to be taking photos, that's illegal. I'm not about to lose the chance of working with them, so right there I opened the back of the camera, ripped out the film and said there ya go, not a bit of harm done. Better all the way round that way. Old Ofeelia had a bit of a fit when I whispered to her as they were all traipsing out of the dining room, but that's life isn't it? She left me alone with the cleaning tonight, but I'll be damned if there wasn't another boatload of sugar in her pockets and even some of it stuffed down those long blue socks.

There's a new magazine out that has all sorts of stuff about the films. There I was looking at a picture of Daniel Day Lewis in his Mohican rigout and who walks in but Dolores in her nursing whites, giving me all sorts of shit for not doing my job right. Slaps the magazine right out of my hands. Look who's talking, I wanted to say. In there in the kitchen nattering about the patients all night long. And sleeping on the job too. Saw her later on in the kitchen with the other nurses, slobbering all over the magazine. They all think that Day Lewis fella is gorgeous. I'll grow my hair long, get a number done on my teeth, and get a job in Hollywood myself. Watch out boys, here come Marty Lyons with his hatchet flying.

Anyway, Ofeelia came waltzing down the corridors when I was mopping at half past four and said to me, *Some night let's go for a walk outside, you and me, for a breath of fresh air.* Didn't say a thing, just kept on mopping. She's fucking bonkers if she thinks I'm going to go for a stroll with her. She asked me for more syrup too, but I didn't say a thing. I was thinking of asking her for that eighty-six pence, but I didn't.

Barney left in his application with the mining boys today. Looking for a man to do the JCB, he said. Told them he worked for the County Council for seven bloody years before he went to the bin. So up I go myself to fill one in too. Place is fierce nice inside—done it up awful posh, expensive carpet and all that lark. Fax machines ringing like bloody Wall Street or something. They fixed the hole in the roof where the telescope used to be. Ah well, that's progress. Three-piece asked me if I'd ever done the bulldozer thing before, so I told him the truth. Told me, natural as could be, that he already has a few men with experience but he'll keep me on file. Bastard like that.

needs a lobotomy if he thinks Barney is telling the truth. That's what you get, though. Doors slammed in your mush when you do it honest.

Georgie and Ofeelia were bulling today when they couldn't go for a walk in the rain. I got in at five o'clock and there they were, in the dining room, sitting away from everyone, scowling like the clappers. Ofeelia had a fucking field of sugar in her pockets, you'd swear she'd been pulling beets all day. Georgie was rocking like a madwoman. Seems they're pals now. Maybe Ofeelia's shooting the white stuff, who knows around this bloody place. Both of them whispering and pointing the finger at me, of all people. Then they started laughing. One thing's for sure, Barney better stop with this Hamlet shite or I'll rip his head off and leave a long slimy one down his throat. He better be half decent to me or I'll up and tell the mining company, not a bother on me, and that's the fucking truth.

This place is driving me around the bend. Geraldine Mc-Cabe was slapped in the solitary after swallowing her fucking thermometer. Una Harrison's parents left her a box of Milk Tray after six o'clock visit and Maggie the Moaner ate them up. All because the lady loves Milk Tray, I suppose. Mary Marshall left another jam rag in the toilet tank. Barney left it for me to clean up, the lazy pillock.

Two weeks now she's been here and she's awful nice. I don't think she's as mad as half the bloody people in the country. She must be a cute hoor to be able to slip past the nurses at night. Down she comes and sits near where I'm working whispering about this that and the other, the price of butter, whatever you want. One night she's talking about things a little wacky, like how the universe is expanding and some such shite about gravity and stuff. Then she's just staring away at the wall. The next she's on about the flowers down by the pond, straight and narrow as could be, a little bit of a twitch in the lip but that's all. It must be said that there's a little bit of a tinkle in the trousers every now and then, what with her in that dressing gown with the buttons open and that bit of nipple looking like a crater on the moon. She's got these awful big lips. Very sexy that in a woman. And those rhododendrons don't look too bad. A man could go blind afterward. I'm surprised Barney doesn't wear glasses after what he does in the stock room.

We've started taking to walks every now and then, me and Ofeelia. Nothing happens, just walking down around the grounds, but the Barney is like a fucking tape recorder. *Hey, Hamlet, did you go for your midnight snack? D'ya think she could suck a golf ball through a fifty foot hose on a windy Friday?* I swear that bastard's looking for a punch, but he's a big one. Might have to take my breakfast and lunch with me. He'll be off and about soon enough working with the suits up there at the mining company, flinging his bulldozer around. Still and all, he's probably right about me getting booted if they find me out walking in the grounds with Ofeelia. Not very clever, he says, even for you. All we do is go out the back door with my key, take our shoes off when we go across the gravel, go down to the flower beds, and she looks at them. Every now and then she picks one and sticks it in her hair.

Better be careful, but she asked me to take her along towards the caboose tomorrow night. I told her that maybe it wasn't a good idea. She says why. I'm not into telling her about the churners and all, but I tell her a little about how I didn't get the bulldozer job. She says she knew about the dozers and that's all right she just wants to see it. Goes on about the homesick lark again, and something weird about her driving the caboose through the universe with her old man. That's madness if you ask me. Seeing how it's propped up on cement blocks, I don't think it's going anywhere soon. But I said alright, maybe we'll take a wander up there one night but we better not get caught or it's my arse on a string. Then she winks at me and asks me not to tell a soul, those flowers bobbing away. She's not too pally with Georgie anymore for some reason and says she doesn't like Barney at all. Was awful happy when I told her he was quitting, but I didn't tell her what job he was taking. She's had enough shite thrown at her these last few weeks.

By all accounts they're going looney trying to get her to go to the dentist. She opened up her gob and showed me a huge hole in the back of her mouth where the molars should be. That's from eating too much sugar I says, and she starts laughing like a bloody hyena. Says she tucks the yellow boys in there with her tongue when the doctors give them to her. Hides them away. She'll be fucked if they're going to dope her up to the gills. She's not thick, Ofeelia. Bet she saw that in a movie somewhere. Tom bloody Cruise in the stars again maybe.

Fucking Dolores and her hawk eyes. Out we were in the corridors talking about taking our stroll and along she comes, in her whites, and reams me out for talking with the patients. Ofeelia goes slinking back to the dorm, a look as long as the Shannon on her mush. Dolores says she's going to tell the big boys if I ever do something like that again. Every day she's Miss Up-your-Arse about every fucking thing, clean the floors, wash the sinks, the storeroom needs bloody cleaning. Sometimes I have the urge to tell her about Barney wanking in there but what's the point. The fucker's leaving in a few days to work on that road for the mining boys and before you know it he'll be wearing a Louis Copeland and driving a Beemer. Phoned them myself again today but they said employment's on hold for now. Some fucking good that does me.

Sometimes I think about Ofeelia and maybe getting a kiss or two one night. If she doesn't mind the teeth and all. I've been thinking about getting braces one of these days. I'll tell the dentist that story about Ofeelia and the yellow boys. That'll crack the bastard up. Maybe he'll give me a discount.

Trial run, she called it. Thank God Dolores had a day off. And Barney is finished, a couple of days off to get ready for the job he says. I said no at first. It's getting a bit dicey. But she hands me one of those flowers again and a man can't refuse that, can he.

Out we slipped at half past two and it's one hell of a fucking hike up to the caboose, around and down by Martin's place, then up the road where Barney's JCB will be doing the trick. Wind blowing in from the sea and all. Had to give her my coat and up she comes and pecks me on the cheek, telling me I'm awful sweet. Like sugar, I say, and she laughs. We scooted around the side of the barbed wire and there was a light in the window behind the curtains. Sat ourselves down in the heather on the hillside. Security man probably doing the same thing Barney gets up to.

Got a bit of a tear in her eye even when she looked at the place, Ofeelia did. Talking about the flower beds and all. Used to be there wasn't a piece of machinery in sight, only that telescope poking out of the roof. Sometimes she'd play hide-and-seek with her mother under the caboose. Got very fucking strange at one point, though, and started saying things from the Bible, all messed around. *Yea though I walk through the valley of the shadow of death I shall fear no evil for I have the biggest fucking JCBs in the valley.* Just like that, her lip twitching. But then she says sorry, I'm just upset, and started talking normal again, reaching up for the flowers going berserk on her head.

Found out about the driving through the universe. Seems her Da used to play a game or two where they'd sit on the bloody roof and pretend they were driving the carriage through the stars. Weird that. They'd pretend they were train drivers just scooting around the sky.

Awful clever about the names of things though, she is. Told her all I knew was the Plough but she had a list as long as your bloody arm. There's one called Betelgeuse and I knew that from the film. But there's others you couldn't pronounce even if you went to university. Seems her old dear would get a bit upset when her father got rude, parked the caboose in O'Ryan's groin or through the legs of the Gemini sisters. But most of all they just had fun, she said, pretending they were driving, blowing the horn as they drove past Mars. Had me cracking up, she did, all that talk about stars. O'Ryan's the bloke with the big sword. And Venus is the one for love, she said. And it's a grand old bright one too.

We were going to do a bit of the driving game ourselves there on the hillside, but I looked at my bloody watch and it was almost four and we had to run back to the bin like the clappers. Was hankering for a bit of slap bang wallop but there was no time at all. She bummed a cigarette off me before she went back to the dorm, but I'm going to have to give those fucking things up because I was wheezing like a horse after running and then scrubbing the place down. Strange that, the way she said it was a trial run. I'll be fucked if I'm going back there. Simple as that. And I'm not getting any more syrup either, even though she asked for four bottles and gave me a tenner. Seems she's back in with Georgie because she said she'd be coming for the stroll too. I said no fucking way, count me out of this lark, I'll be scrubbing the floors, no ifs, ands, or buts, Georgie girl's as mad as a fucking hatter.

Johnnie Logan's on about the miners again. There he is, his photo plastered all over the newspapers. Says the land belonged to others before it was ours, now we're giving it away again. Can't see much sense in that since there's no Brits running around these parts these days. Still and all he's talking like the clappers about the empire and multi-something companies and all that stuff. Johnnie Boy should have a go at Hollywood.

I was sitting in the town square listening to him run his mouth off and thinking about old Ofeelia and the way she'd take a flying trip on the damn thing. That must have been a sight. Then I got to thinking that maybe Logan is right. Maybe they should fuck off back to Ballyfermot and leave our mountains alone. Then again if they gave me a job I'd kick the living daylights out of Logan and never vote for the pillock again. Told Ofeelia that I'd make one more trip up there with her if Georgie didn't come along. She says ah go on, but I said no way José. She was biting away at her lip for a while, but then just gave me a goozer and said okay, no Georgie. This time she gave me one quick smack on the lips. Boys oh boys talk about the rise of the empire. Johnnie Logan would have said a thing or two if he'd seen my trousers.

All settled so. Ofeelia wants me to take a wire cutters, a hammer, and a screwdriver from the storeroom. Says she just wants to go up and touch the caboose again. Just get through the barbed wire and touch the damn thing with her fingers. I'll go along. I don't give a shite. Barney was in the Humbert today telling people I'd become a fucking patient. He was quoting something about to be or not to be. That smart arse is looking for his comeuppance. Him up there on the dozers making money hand over fist. It was pissing rain tonight so we didn't go outside, me and Ofeelia. Found a flower down behind the toilet bowl though.

Another fucking delay. It was pissing rain again tonight. Ofeelia went barmy with the sugar. Christ that girl's definitely off her rocker. Now that Barney's gone there's twice as much bloody work around the bin.

Christ. I don't know if a man can actually say what happens to him if he tries to drive through the stars. But it must be a fucking beautiful trip, that's all I have to say.

Got up to the bin at five bells, like always, and got to mopping the corridors, almost clean fucking forgot about our trip to the caboose and all. But out she comes from the dining room and says can we go for our stroll tonight. None of the nurses looking and she sort of takes my hand. *Thank you very much,* she says, straightforward as can be, a look on her that'd melt you. Polished the place to a bloody shine I did all night, just leaning into the mop like a lunatic, scrubbing all the water spots off the mirrors, taking all the stuff out of the dustbins, fixing the towels, cleaning the toilets, mopping the floors so they sparkled just like in the telly ads. Could have shaved myself by looking in that floor, I swear to God. Was finished triple bloody quick.

Dolores had been on the piss the night before and looking no better than a burned-out saucepan. She was having a nap in the nurse's station when out Ofeelia comes, all done up to the nines. Her hair was back from her eyes, six rhododendrons going hell for leather, and a bit of makeup here and there. She was wearing a long red dress and the biggest bloody hiking boots I've ever seen in my life. She had four Dunnes Stores bags in her hands, weighed down like mad so she was almost walking sideways. I whispered to her what the fuck is in the bags, Ofeelia. And she asks what did you call me. So I says nothing, just a nickname. But she nearly went barmy trying to get it out of me. So I told her what Barney called her and all, and she took out the flowers and trampled them on the bloody floor. I almost gave her a good box for messing up all my hard work, but there were all these tears in her eyes and all I did was get the sweeping brush and swept all the petals into the storeroom.

I said are we right, let's go, and asked her again what was in the bags. I almost shit myself when I saw all that sugar, dumped out from the sachets, a huge mound of the stuff. The other bag was chock-full of the bloody syrup bottles. I asked her what she was bringing them for, but she just gave me a shrug and said right we are, we're on our way. I had the cutters, the hammer, and the screwdriver in a red Man United bag with a picture of Paul McGrath on the side, even though he's playing now for Villa. McGrath's face was peeling a bit from where I put it in the washing machine by mistake years ago. We were bloody quiet getting out of there, taking off our shoes as we went across the gravel, then laced them up again and went toward the trees. She was humming something or other as we went down to the main gate. Every time we saw a few cars, in we ducked to the bushes and hid. Once she ran her fingers through my hair and I thought there and then about that Chris de Burgh song about the lady in red, which is a stupid fucking song but gets the women all horny. But there was no time for any of that. She did give me a goozer, though, a long slow one with her tongue almost halfway down my throat. I was wondering about the teeth but she didn't say a thing. I could hardly walk straight after that one.

When we got down to the caboose road we could hear the sea. Ofeelia stopped and had a goo at the sky for a few minutes. There was all stone walls and grass around there, like in the Saw Doctors song. There was no moon out but I swear there was a rim of light around her hair from the stars, stupid and all as it sounds. I felt like singing her a verse or two. But we heard a badger scuttling away through the bushes, which frightened the shite out of both of us, and then we just lugged our stuff up the road. I was carrying the sugar and the Man United bag and it was heavy as all get-out. There was a light in the caboose window as normal. Four of the dozers were outside, yellow as could be. There were a few charred oil barrels, a cement churner, one of those huge roller machines and a blue Bedford Van with the mining company insignia on the side, the wheels all shiny. Not the way Bedford vans are supposed to be. Not in this neck of the woods anyway.

We circled on around the back, along the barbed wire fence, and stopped for a while in the heather. There was a fishing boat with lights on out in the sea. It wasn't too cold at all. *Trust me,* she said. *Don't do anything stupid.* Fair enough said I, and I knew we were up to a hell of a lot more than just touching that fucking caboose. But I didn't care.

Down we scrambled, to the bottom of the hill, like Steve McQueen escaping from that prison. Christ, I never felt so good. Got a hole in the Dunnes Stores sugar bag and had to hold the fucker by both ends so it didn't spill out. Out with the wire cutters and she's watching me with those big green eyes like a cat as we go snippety-snip and in like rabbits through the fence. What the fuck we going to do now, I says to her. She just puts her finger to those big lips and waves her arms towards the bloody bulldozer. Along we crawl, just like in the films, that red dress of hers getting awful muddy.

The heart almost fucking leapt out of me when I saw the security guard's shadow move in the caboose, but the wanker didn't show. Under the bulldozer we got and I'll be fucked if Ofeelia didn't start reaching up into the huge bloody engine

164

and start clipping every wire in sight. Christ the woman was around the bend and back again. I was getting a bit of a kick out of it, it must be said, and started to reach up into the engine too, thinking fuck you Barney me boy, see if you can make a few bob now, and where the hell is your three-piece suit anyway. Then, by Christ, there looks likes there's a million fucking wires hanging down like bloody decorations.

I miss this place, she says to me. *Used to be we had a great time up here.* I nod my head. I know how you feel, says I. I had a bicycle once that got nicked when I was eight and the mother slapped me for crying. She starts whispering about her old man and how he was making a map of the sky out of Irish stories, like Cuchulainn and Diarmuid and Grainne and all. That'd be a funny fucking map, I says, the salmon of knowledge leaping out of your man's hands. I pointed up at O'Ryan, who was lower in the sky than he was the other night. She was laughing until I told her to shut up, we'll get caught. She smiled at me awful long until I says come on let's get cracking.

Ofeelia never counted on me being a dab hand with a lock, though. Up she gets with a screwdriver and the hammer and stands at the back of the JCB, whispering to me to knock the fucking petrol cap off for some reason. I tell her she's fucking nuts, we should just pick the thing, otherwise the security guard would think this was O'Connell Street with all the noise. I've been doing that sort of thing since I was knee-high to a grasshopper. So out comes the old trusty nail file that I carry everywhere, swear to God. Ofeelia's happy as Larry. Those locks on the petrol tanks are a curse though and I had to use a little piece of metal that I filed down a long time ago but eventually she popped out good-oh. That was a fucking brand new JCB as well.

Ofeelia took out the sugar and started pouring the stuff in the tank like it was going out of fashion. I heard about that somewhere but forgot. Fucks up the engine no end, a bit of sugar. No wonder she'd been robbing it. Ofeelia had no end of tricks, the yellow boys and the sugar and all. Some of it spilled out on the ground, but most of it went down the gob of the machine.

She was humming the tune about a spoonful of sugar and the medicine going down when out hops the fucking security guard with his torch shining. Ofeelia stands stock still and I fall to the ground. He looks around a bit, lifts his right leg in the air, farts, and steps back into the caboose. I almost die laughing and Ofeelia she has a smile on her face to beat the band. Then she gets out the syrup, something I never heard about before, and dumps two bottles of the stuff in there. She tells me it'll clog up the engine even if they get the wires fixed. That and the sugar will really do a number. The boys won't move that dozer up the mountain for many a year, I tell her, but already she's scrambling off to the other one. She drops the syrup bottle on the ground. Litterbug, I says and her still smiling.

Out she pops with a coathanger from the syrup bag, with the end all sharpened to a point, and she reaches right up into the engine with those small hands. It seems like all fucking night as she punctures something or other. She knows these fucking engines inside out. All this petrol starts pouring out and it gets all over her red dress. Damn, she's soaked in the stuff. In her hair and everything. I get in there and drag her out and the stuff does a number on me too. Stinks to high heaven the petrol does and she's doused in the stuff, but so what. We were getting the job done triple quick. Then it's another number on the wires of the second JCB, my hands shaking like fucking mad. Christ, this is living, I think. Johnnie Logan and the greenies would love me. I should run for fucking Taoiseach after this. Out with the spoonful of sugar again. *In the most delightful way*, she says. Then some more syrup.

Up to the Bedford, which is open, so I pop the bonnet. Ofeelia she's just standing there, smiling, looking up at the stars. But then there's a clink at the caboose door and that bastard is out again, shining his bloody light, catching her in the beam and it's all fucking hell let loose. Must have heard me messing with the Bedford. Out he steps, shining the fucker in Ofeelia's eyes. I'm about to run but Ofeelia she's stepping towards him and swinging her arms like a bloody windmill. It's John O'Rourke who once slapped me around in school. She lands a good old thump on his jaw, but he gets Ofeelia by the hair and drags her down, shouting fucking bitch scraped me face. He's in his vest and trousers. Some fucking security guard that.

I step over and clock him one with the hammer. Didn't mean to do that and down he drops with blood on his face, oh Christ. I kneel down and he's all right, just cut him to fuck over the eyebrow. I'm about to say I didn't mean it Johnnie me boy, when he knees me one in the balls and kicks me in the head as I'm down. Times don't change. Ofeelia she's hanging off his back in the red dress and I'm half-out for the count. Next thing I know he's scarping away, out over the fence and away. Ofeelia, she's laughing and crying at the same time, and there's a mad bitch if ever I saw one. *They took my caboose,* she's saying, real real low, *they took my caboose.* The makeup around her eyes is streaked like mad. I go up and give her a hug and she gets to kissing my eyes, just like that. I sit down on the ground and just look around, and she kneels and keeps kissing. The red dress is brown as hell now. I see John O'Rourke's torch shining away down the hill, lashing along through the bushes towards Martin's place. The bastard'll call the cops, I said, let's skedaddle.

The door to the caboose was open though and Ofeelia was staring at it, standing there, stinking of petrol. Christ, I'm thinking, she's off her rocker and beyond, Doctor Garlic should have kept her in solitary, and we'd all be grand now, scrubbing the toilet bowls and mopping the floors without a fucking care. Come on! I'm shouting, for Christ sake come on! *It's all right I'll finish it now,* she says. Just like that. *On my own.* Calm as can be. My hands are shaking like mad and I go to drag her by the dress but she's awful quick and takes a sidestep. *Please,* she says, sad as can be, hair all over her face. Ah Christ, I think we were standing there for hours, her just looking at me. All right so, I say, don't tell the cops it was me, that O'Rourke fella didn't get a look at my face. She nods her head and turns to the caboose, closes the door awful gentle like and I take the hammer and sling it as far as I bloody can, but it bounces off the barbed-wire fence and jumps a bit on the ground. I look up at the sky and let out a big gullier at the stars.

Right so, I says to myself, and off I go towards the hole in the fence and my hands still shaking like mad. She can get out of this fucking mess herself. Out I crawl and just lash through the heather up the side of the hill. I don't look back for the longest time, just run up there, blazing away like Eamon Coughlan himself. After a while I sit down, take myself a place on the hill, petrol stink on my hands, and look way down towards the town, where these red-and-blue sirens are blaring like fuck, coming out towards us. I squint my eyes and see Ofeelia through the front window of the caboose.

She's just sitting there and smiling for some damn reason. Her hair is thrown back and the dress is ripped at the shoulder, but she's just sitting there, watching. Bet the crazy bitch is driving that damn thing through the stars, I'm thinking. Up I stand and give her a big thumbs-up. Go on now girl, get yourself a speeding ticket! Give it an old handbrake turn! She just looks up at the huge sky up there and all the stars blazing away. I look up there too for a moment and think about all those times she might have been there with her old man, driving through the universe like fucking crazy, O'Ryan's groin and all, that must have been a laugh.

I can hear the sound of the ocean and the wind going mad through the heather. There's a million bloody stars out and I'm enjoying the view, but the sirens are getting closer. Better get the fuck out of here now, I'm thinking. Back and scrub the floors like bejesus. Those blue-and-red lights are flashing away down the road, along by the trees. Oh Christ she's done for now. I look down and Ofeelia's still sitting there, her eyes scrunched up, that smile on her face. But there's not much they can do except throw her back in the bin, and I'm thinking that maybe every now and then, if things work out, we'll get a chance to go for a walk in the garden. I give her the old thumbs-up again. How about you put her up on two bloody wheels Ofeelia! Screech her round the corner of Venus and leave some skidmarks for your Ma and Da, why not! See you soon and don't be asking me for any more syrup!

There's nothing I could have done anyway even when she sat there at the window and put that cigarette in her gob and lit it. By all accounts she had popped those yellow boys like they were going out of fashion while I was climbing the hill, so maybe she didn't feel a thing, all doped up. That's what the coroner said anyway. She must have had them with her in her pocket. But I don't think I ever ran as fast in my life when I saw her take out those matches. Reached down into her pocket, looked at them, took one out, struck it and that was it. The guards say I was screaming her name. Cut myself to fuck on the barbed wire. Tripped once and slammed into the door. She had locked the fucker and by the time I pulled it open she was a ball of flames, sitting there, all that petrol from the JCB lit up like a bonfire.

She bummed that fucking cigarette off me and that's something I'll never forget. I once saw pictures of a monk doing the same thing, but I've never seen anything like that in my life. Just licking away at the red dress, the flames were. And beginning to gather around her. Her stock-still in the middle of it all. Tried to roll her out but the flames got to me too, burning the shit out of my hands and the guards had to rip all my clothes off. Barney said that he heard I was crying, but I don't take any truck with Barney any more. The bastard's back working at the bin, and there's no more JCBs for him, serves him right.

I don't even care if I was crying or not, who cares. But I know I was shouting something because one of the guards slapped me in the gob and told me to shut up. Christ, she was charred black at that stage and there they were, stamping the flames out around the caboose. It's just an awful pity that whole fucking place never caught, that's what I say. There were some scorch marks around the floor and her big hiking boots were black as fuck, but the place was still standing when they took me away in the ambulance. They tried to get me to lie down but there was no fucking way. I was looking at the caboose out the back of the window for as long as I could, all lit up by cop cars and fire engines and all.

Here in the hospital they've been looking after my burns and filing all sorts of reports and all. Johnnie Logan and the greenies came in with a bunch of flowers for me, pink ones just like Ofeelia's. Dolores brought me a few magazines, fair play to her. The cops are taking me to court next week and I'll probably spend a couple of months in the slammer. I don't care. I'll be quiet as a mouse. Then when I get out I swear to God I'm going to do a number on that caboose, up and make sure those mining boys never come back, off to fucking Timbuktu with them for all I care. One good thing about it is we knocked their plans back a good few months but they need to be finished off, pronto like. Stay away from our fucking mountains, that's what I say.

The cops and the doctors have been asking me all about it, but all I can really remember is that when they were slamming the handcuffs on me I saw a picture of Ofeelia in my mind, and when I get to thinking about it that picture always comes back to me. And it's always the same. It isn't the crumple on the floor or anything, or that Dunnes Stores bag lying out by the JCBs or the flower beds or anything. It isn't even real. She doesn't have the cigarette in her gob or matches in her hands. It's like something in a film I suppose. The way I see it she has flowers in her hair, dozens of them, wrapped up in the curls, and she's sitting there, bloody pink petals flying, driving that damn caboose through the universe for the last time, smiling like the clappers, going hell for leather along by the stars. And the funny thing about it is I'm right there with her, leaving a few bloody skidmarks of my own.

ALONG THE RIVERWALL

Fergus nudges his wheelchair up to the riverwall and watches the Liffey flow quickly along, bloated from an evening rain, a cargo of night sky and neon, all bellying down toward Dublin bay. His father once heaved a fridge into the river and he wonders what else might lie down there. Flakes of gold paint from the Guinness barges perhaps. Blackened shells from British army gunboats. Condoms and needles. Old black kettles. Pennies and prams. History books, harmonicas, fingernails, and baskets full of dead flowers. A billion cigarette butts and bottle caps. Shovels and stovepipes, coins and whistles, horseshoes and footballs. And many an old bicycle, no doubt. Down there with wheels sinking slowly in the mud, handlebars galloping with algae, gear cables rusted into the housing, tiny fish nosing around the pedals.

He adjusts the long black overcoat that hangs in anarchic folds around his legs and wipes the sweat off his forehead with his younger brother's Shamrock Rovers scarf. Half a mile, he reckons, from his house in the Liberties, and the bicycle wheel that he carried in his lap has caused all sorts of problems—dropped to the ground as he gently tried to close the front door, smeared his old jeans with a necklace of oil as he negotiated the hill down by Christchurch, and bounced away as he tried to get over the quayside curb.

The Liffey guides a winter wind along its broad-backed banks. Fergus puts the brake on the wheelchair and lets a gob of phlegm volley out over the river, where it catches and spirals. He wonders what sort of arc the bicycle wheel will make in the air.

The fridge, all those years ago, tumbled head over heels into the water. His father, a leather-faced man with pockets always full of bottles, had taken it down to the river all on his own. He hadn't been able to keep up the payments and wasn't ready to hand it back to the collector. "That gouger can go for a swim if he wants his Frigidaire." He nailed a few planks from the coal shed together, screwed some rollerskate wheels on the bottom, loaded up the fridge, and grunted down toward the quays. Fergus and his brothers tagged behind. Some of the drunks who were belching out of the pubs offered help, but Fergus's father flung his arms in the air. "Every single one of ya is a horse of a man," he roared, then stopped and pulled on his cigarette, "but yez can't shit walking, so I'll do it meself."

Bottles clinking, he stumbled down to the river, laughing as the huge white fridge cartwheeled into the water, creating a gigantic splash.

The things that fridge must have joined, thinks Fergus. Broken toilets. Flagons of cider. Shirt buttons. High-heeled shoes.

A very old pair of crutches. He shivers for a moment in the cold and runs his fingers around through his short curly hair. Or perhaps even a rotating bed, flanked with special syringes, piss bags, rubber gloves, buckets of pills, bottles of Lucozade, a dozen therapy tables, a nurse's pencil with the ends chewed off. Holding onto the axle and the freewheel, Fergus spins the spokes around, peers through them, and listens to the rhythmic click as the river and the quays tumble into slices, then lets another volley from his throat out over the water.

Mangled by a bread truck on the Lansdowne Road, near where the Dodder negotiates low rocks. Bucketfuls of winter sun coming down as he rode back from a delivery, over the bridge by the football stadium, inventing Que Seras and Molly Malones and Ronnie Whelan hitting an eighteen-yard volley from the edge of the box. But there was only a song of tires and the poor bastard behind the wheel of the bread truck had a heart attack and was found with eclair cream on the front of his white open-neck shirt, brown loaves littered around him on the floor, slumped frontward on the truck horn, so that it sounded like the cry of a curlew, only constant, with blood in a pattern of feathers on the front windshield.

Fergus was tossed in the air like a stale crust and woke up in Our Lady of Lourdes Rehabilitation Center with the doctors in a halo around him. Collarbone broken, thirty forehead stitches, ribs cracked, and the third lumbar on the lower vertebrae smashed to hell. He was put in a ward full of rugby players and motorcycle victims. When his bed was spun he could see out the window to a ripple of trees that curtsied down to the road. Weeks rivered like months. A Cavanman in the bed beside him had a pair of scars that ran like railroad tracks when he held his wrists together. A persistent howl thudded down from the end of the ward. A carrot-haired boy from Sligo tattooed a tricolor on the top of his leg, slamming the needle down hard into a muscle that didn't feel a thing. The months eddied carelessly into one another.

"How d'ya think I feel, I'm marvelous, just fuckin' marvelous," Fergus roared at the nurse one afternoon when the knowledge was settling in—no more slipstreaming the 45 bus down Pearse Street in the rain or sprinting along by the brewery, slapping at dogs with the bicycle pump, dicing the taxis, swerving the wrong way up the street, no more jokes about women sitting on things other than the crossbar—*that's not my crossbar, love, I'm only happy to see ya*—or slagging matches along the quays with the truck drivers, or simply just trundling down Thomas Street for a pint of milk.

The bike was at home in the coal shed, a trophy of misery, collected by his father on the day of the accident. He had bought it for Fergus five years before, convinced that his son was good enough to race. Every payday he had rolled up his spare pound notes and stuffed them inside a Pernod bottle. He brought the bike home one Saturday night, carefully wheeling it from the shop on George's Street. It was a red Italian model, all Camagnolo parts. Boys in the neighborhood whistled when they saw it. Once, on O'Connell Bridge, four youngsters in bomber jackets tried to knock him off and steal it, but he smacked one in the jaw with the kryptonite lock. In the messenger company he was known for the way he salmoned, leaping through the traffic the wrong way up a one-way road. In his first race, in the Wicklow Hills, two months before the accident, he had come in second place. The leather on the saddle had begun to conform to his body. He had learned how to flick it quite easily through the traffic jams up by Christchurch.

After the accident the machine was a ribbon of metal. But, when his father came into the hospital, he would tower over the bed: "Before y'know it, Fergus, you'll be on her again, and fuck all the begrudgers." Fergus lay there, nodding.

His mother stayed upstairs in her bedroom, kneeling by red votive lamps and holy pictures. Letters were sent off to Knock and Lourdes. His younger brothers drew pictures of favorite places, Burdocks Chipper, the alleyway down by the Coombe, the front of the Stag's Head, the new graffiti on the schoolyard wall. Fergus's friends from the messenger service sat by the hospital bed and sometimes they'd race off together, radios crackling, *come on ya tosser would ya hurry up for fuck sake.* Old girlfriends wrote short poems that they found in magazines, and occasionally the nurses brought him down to Baker's Corner for a sweet and furtive pint. But when the bed was spun the same trees curtsied down to the road. The boy with the tricolor went berserk with the pins, covering himself in small blue dots and stabbing at his eye with a needle. The Cavanman stroked his wrists. A biker from Waterford shouted that someone had left a pubic hair in the French magazine that had circulated around the ward. Oranges gathered mold on Fergus's bedside table. The therapy room was full of bright colors and smiling nurses, but at night, back in the ward, the distant low moan wouldn't subside—it became part of the scenery, swallowed up, a hum, a drone, a noise you couldn't sleep without. The months flowed on.

Home from the hospital, his father wheeled him out to the coal shed. It was a Friday and fish was being cooked in the house. The smell drifted. A light drizzle was falling and pigeons were scrapping for food on the rooftops of neighboring houses. His father opened the lock of the shed slowly. Half a dozen brown boxes waited for Fergus, beside the bicycle. They'd been postmarked in England, sent by mail order. Fergus opened them slowly. "The doctors don't know their arses from their elbows, son, go on ahead there now and get cracking." Fergus stared at the boxes for a long time. "And they cost a lot fucking more than a miracle," said his father, chuckling, heading out the door toward the pub, his shoulders ripping at the side of his overcoat. Fergus sat there, the smell of cooking food all around him, fingering a derailleur.

Hitching the scarf up around his neck, he looks at his watch—already three o'clock in the morning—and then lays his head back against the edge of the wheelchair for a moment to look up to the sky. Certain stars are recognizable even through the clouds and the smog. Ten years ago, when he was seven years old, he'd been caught trying to steal a Mini Clubman from outside St. Patrick's, and his father, after walloping him, took him for a walk down the same river, pointing up at the sky. "See those stars," he said, "let me tell ya something." The story was that the stars were their own peculiar hell, that all the murderers went to one star where there was nobody left to murder but themselves, all the corrupt politicians went where there was no government, all the child molestors went where there were no children to molest, all the car thieves went where there were no cars, and if that wasn't good enough deterrent for him, he'd get another wallop. Fergus rubs his hand over his chest and wonders if there's a star full of bicycle paraphernalia.

The new parts had cost his father the best part of two wage packets. He had even gotten an extra job as a night watchman for a security firm in Tallaght. When he came home at night there wasn't so much as a clink inside his pockets anymore—it was more a persistent clatter of dismissive humphs, an emphatic hope, a nagging insistence that Fergus would get on the bike again.

And out in the coal shed, for two months, in the wheelchair, Fergus sweated over the bicycle. He tightened the nipples of the spokes on the right hand side of the wheel to bring it to the left, took the cotter pin and tapped it until the fat leap came out of the pedals, used the third hand to hold the brakes in place, dropped in the new set of front forks, plied the thin little Phillips-head screwdriver to adjust the gears. He overlapped the tape on the handlebars, twisted the ends of the cables where they frayed, bought new decals. His brothers watched and helped. Each night his father would come out to the coal shed, slap the saddle: "Just a few weeks now, son."

He offered the bike to his brothers, but they knew better. It was a fossil, and Fergus knew it, and the only thing it could be ridden with was a perfect cadence of the imagination.

First to go were the handlebars and they went down with a small splash. The following night the pedals, the cranks, the front chainwheel, and the ball bearings were tossed. It was a Saturday when he wandered down to jettison the brakes, the cables, the saddle, the seatpost, and the derailleur. A crowd of drunks were huffing glue down on the quays, so he sat in the gateway of the Corporation building and waited until they drifted off.

Sunday was the most difficult job of all—it had taken three hours to try and negotiate the frame, and he was about to just leave it alongside the church when a taxi driver, with a cigarette dangling from his mouth, pulled alongside him and asked what the hell he was doing. "Bringing the bike for a swim," said Fergus, and the driver just nodded, then offered to put it in the boot and drive it down to the river for him. He balanced the frame on the riverwall. "Just as well this isn't the bleedin' Ganges," said the driver, and drove off. Fergus, unsure of what the taxi man meant, toppled the frame over the wall and headed home, not even waiting for the ripples to spread out over the water.

And last night, when he went to get rid of the front wheel, he woke his brother Padraic as the door of the coal shed swung too far. Padraic came downstairs in his Arsenal jersey: "Wha' ya doin', Ferg?" "Mind your own business." "Where's the rest of the bike?" Fergus said nothing. "Da'll cream ya," said his brother. Later, as Fergus maneuvred down the street, he saw Padraic pull back the curtains and stare. When he got home Padraic was waiting for him on the steps of the house. "Ya've no fucking right to do that," Padraic said. "Da spent all his money on it."

Fergus pushed past his brother into the house: "He'll find out soon enough."

Down along the quays things are still quiet. The exhaust fumes from a couple of trucks make curious shapes in the air, sometimes caught in midflight with a streak of neon from a shop or a sign. A couple of pedestrians stroll along on the opposite side of the river, huddled under anorak hoods.

He bends forward in the chair, grabs one of the spokes, and hauls the rear wheel up to his chest. He sees a smidgin of oil and dirt on the third cog of the freewheel and runs his finger along it. He daubs the oil on the inside of his jeans, staring at the small smudge the oil makes against the blue.

The water is calmer now, with bits of litter settling on its surface. He wonders if all the pieces that he has flung in over the last few days have settled in the same area of river bottom.

Perhaps one day a storm might blow the whole bike back together again, a freak of nature, the pedals locking on to the cranks, the wheel axle slipping into the frame, the handlebars dropping gently into the housing, the whole damn thing back in one piece. Maybe then he can take a dive to the bottom of the slime and ride it again, slip his feet in the toeclips, curl his fingers around the bars, lean down to touch the gears forward, then pedal all around the river bottom, amongst the ruin of things.

He heaves the wheel out over the Liffey.

It flares out over the river, then almost seems to stop. The wheel appears suspended there in the air, caught by a fabulous lightness, the colors from along the quays whirling in its spin, collecting energy from the push of the sky, reeling outward, simultaneously serene and violent, a bird ready to burst into flight. For a moment, he thinks of marathons and jerseys, sprints and headbands, tracks and starting guns. Out there trundling through the traffic of Dublin in a wheelchair, racing along with others, maybe even delivering a package or two, parcels and letters that he can fit in his lap, a small paycheck, his father bending down to look at the money, bottles clanking. His younger brothers at some finishing line in colorful shirts, his mother fingering a string of red beads.

In an instant, the wheel turns sideways and falls. The walls of the Liffey curl up to gather it down to its belly as it slices the air with the economy of a stone. Fergus pins his upper body across the chair, leaning against the wall, but loses sight of the wheel about five feet above the water. He listens for the splash, but it is drowned out by the rumble of a truck coming along the road from the James' Gate Brewery. Down below, on the surface, concentric circles fling themselves outward, reaching for the riverwalls in huge gestures, as if looking for something, galloping outward, the river itself shifting its circles for another moment, moving its whippled water along, all the time gathering the wheel downward to the river floor, slowly, deliberately, to where it will rest. Fergus tries to remember if the door of the fridge had been flung open as it cartwheeled down into the river all those years ago.

He places his hands on the wheels of the chair, grits his teeth, pushes forward along the riverwall, and rams down the quays, his overcoat flapping in the breeze.

CATHAL'S LAKE

It's a sad Sunday when a man has to dig another swan from the soil. The radio crackles and brings Cathal news of the death as he lies in bed and pulls deep on a cigarette, then sighs.

Fourteen years to heaven, and the boy probably not even old enough to shave. Maybe a head of hair on him like a wheat field. Or eyes as blue as thrush eggs. Young, awkward, and gangly, with perhaps a Liverpool scarf tied around his mouth and his tongue flickering into the wool with a vast obscenity carved from the bottom of his stomach. A bottle of petrol in his hands and a rag from his mother's kitchen lit in the top. His arms in the beginnings of a windmill hurl. Then a plastic bullet slamming his chest, all six inches of it hurtling against his lung at one hundred miles an hour. The bottle somersaulting from the boy's fingers. Smashing on the street beneath his back. Thrush eggs broken and rows of wheat going up in flames. The street suddenly quiet and gray as other boys, too late, roll him

185

around in puddles to put out the fire. A bus burning. A pigeon flapping over the rooftops of Derry with a crust of white bread in its mouth. A dirge of smoke breaking into song over the sounds of dustbin lids and keening sirens. And, later, a dozen other bouquets flung relentlessly down the street in memorial milk bottles.

Cathal coughs up a tribute of phlegm to the vision. Ah, but it's a sad Sunday when a man has to go digging again and the lake almost full this year.

He reaches across his bedside table and flips off the radio, lurches out of the bed, a big farmer with a thick chest. The cigarette dangles from his lips. As he walks, naked, toward the window he rubs his balding scalp and imagines the gray street with the rain drifting down on roofs of corrugated iron. A crowd gathering together, faces twitching, angry. The boy still alive in his house of burnt skin. Maybe his lung collapsed and a nurse bent over him. A young mother, her face hysterical with mascara stains, flailing at the air with soapy fists, remembering a page of unfinished homework left on the kitchen table beside a vase of wilting marigolds. Or nasturtiums. Or daisies. Upstairs in his bedroom, a sewing needle with ink on the very tip, where the boy had been tattooing a four-letter word on his knuckles. Love or hate or fuck or hope. The sirens ripping along through the rain. The wheels crunching through glass.

Cathal shivers, pulls aside the tattered curtains and watches a drizzle of rain slant lazily through the morning air, onto the lake, where his swans drift. So many of them out there this year that if they lifted their wings in unison they would all collide together in the air, a barrage of white.

From the farmhouse window Cathal can usually see for miles—beyond the plowed black soil, the jade green fields, the rivulets of hills, the roll of forest, to the distant dun mountains. Today, because of the rain, he can just about make out the lake, which in itself is a miniature country-side—ringed with chestnut trees and brambles, banked ten feet high on the northern side, with another mound of dirt on the eastern side, where frogsong can often be heard. The lake is deep and clear, despite the seepage of manured water from the fields where his cattle graze. On the surface, the swans, with their heads looped low, negotiate the reeds and the waterlilies. The lake can't be seen from the road, half a mile away, where traffic occasionally rumbles.

Cathal opens the window, sticks his head out, lets the cigarette drop, and watches it spiral and fizzle in the wet grass. He looks toward the lake once more.

"Good morning," he shouts. "Have ye room for another?"

The swans drift on, like paper, while the shout comes back to him in a distant echo. He coughs again, spits out the window, closes it, walks to his rumpled bed, pulls on his underwear, a white open-necked shirt, a large pair of dirty overalls, and some wool socks. He trundles slowly along the landing, down the stairs to make his breakfast. All these young men and women dying, he thinks, as his socks slide on the wooden floor. Well, damn it all anyway.

And maybe the soldier who fired the riot gun was just a boy himself. Cathal's bacon fizzles and pops and the kettle lets out a low whistle. Maybe all he wanted, as he saw the boy come forward with the Liverpool scarf wrapped around his mouth, was to be home. Then, as a firebomb whirled through the air, perhaps all the soldier thought of was a simple pint of Watney's. Or a row of Tyneside tenements with a football to bang against the wall. Or to be fastened together with his girlfriend in some little Newcastle alleyway. Perhaps he was wishing that his hair could touch his shoulders, like it used to do. Or that, with the next month's paycheck, he could buy some Afghan hash and sit in the barracks with his friends, blowing rings of Saturn smoke to the ceiling. Maybe his eyes were as deep and green as bottles in a cellar. Perhaps a Wilfred Owen book was tucked under his pillow to make meaning of the whistles on the barbed wire. But there he was, all quivery and trembling, in Londonderry, his shoulder throbbing with the kickback of the gun, looking up to the sky, watching a plume of smoke rise.

Cathal picks the bacon out of the sizzling grease with his fingers and cracks two eggs. He pours himself a cup of tea, coughs, and leaves another gob of phlegm in the sink. The weather has been ferocious this Christmas. Winds that sheer through a body, like a scythe through a scarecrow, have left him with a terrible cold. Not even the Bushmills that he drank last night could put a dent in his chest. What a terrible thought that. He rubs his chest. Bushmills and bullets.

Perhaps, he thinks, a picture of the soldier's girlfriend hangs on the wall above the bunk bed in the barracks. Dog-eared and a little yellow. Her hair all teased and a sultry smile on her face. Enough to make the soldier melt at the knees. Him having to call her, heartbroken, saying: "I didn't mean it, luv. We were just trying to scatter the crowd." Or maybe not. Maybe him with a face like a rat, eyes dark as bogholes, sitting in a pub, glorious in his black boots, being slapped and praised, him raising his glass for a toast, to say: "Did ya see that, lads? What a fucking shot, eh? Newcastle United 1, Liverpool 0."

All this miraculous hatred. Christ, a man can't eat his breakfast for filling his belly full of it. Cathal dips a small piece of bread into the runny yolk of an egg and wipes his chin. In the courtyard some chickens quarrel over scraps of feed. A raven lands on a fence post down by the red barn. Beyond that a dozen cows huddle in the corner of a field, under a tree, sheltering from the rain, which is coming down in steady sheets now. Abandoned in the middle of the field is Cathal's tractor. It gave up the ghost yesterday while he was taking a couple of sacks of oats, grass clippings and cracked corn out to the swans.

Shoveling the last of his breakfast into his mouth, Cathal watches the swans glide lazily across the water, close and tight. Sweet Jesus, but there's not a lot of room left out there these days.

He leaves the breakfast dishes in the sink, unlatches the front door, sits on a wooden stool under the porch roof, and pulls on his green Wellingtons, wheezing. Occasional drops of rain are blown in under the porch and he tightens the drawstrings on his anorak hood. Wingnut, a three-legged collie who lost her front limb when the tractor ran over it, comes up and nestles her head in the crook of Cathal's knee. From his anorak pocket he pulls out a box of cigarettes, cups his hands, and lights up. Time to give these damn things up, he thinks, as he walks across the courtyard, the cigarette crisping and flaring. Wingnut chases the chickens in circles around some puddles, loping around on her three legs.

"Wingnut!"

The dog tucks her head and follows Cathal down toward the red barn. Hay is piled up high in small bales and bags of feed clutter the shelves. Tractor parts are heaped in the corner. A chaotic mess of tools slouches against the wall. Cathal puts his toe under the handle of a pitchfork and, with a flick of the foot, sends it sailing across the barn. Then he lifts a tamping bar, leans it in the corner, and grabs his favorite blue-handled shovel.

Christ, the things a man could be doing now if he wasn't cursed to dig. Could be fixing the distributor cap on the trac-tor. Or binding up the northern fence. Putting some paraffin down that foxhole to make sure that little red-tailed bastard doesn't come hunting chickens any more. Or down there in the southernmost field, making sure the cattle have enough cubes to last them through the cold. Or simply just sitting by the fire having a smoke and watching television, like any decent man fifty-six years old would want to do.

All these years of digging. A man could reach his brother in Australia, or his sister in America, or even his parents in heaven or hell if he put all that digging together into one single hole.

"Isn't that right, Wingnut?" Cathal reaches down and takes Wingnut's front leg and walks her out of the barn, laughing as the collie barks, the shovel tucked under his shoulder.

He moves back through the courtyard again, the dog at his heels. As he walks he whisks the blade of the shovel into the puddles and hums a tune. Wonder if they're singing right now, over the poor boy's body? The burns lightened by cosmetics perhaps, the autumn-colored hair combed back, the eyelids fixed in a way of peace, the mouth bitter and mysterious, the tattooed hand discreetly covered. A priest bickering because he doesn't want a flag draped on the coffin. A sly undertaker saying that the boy deserves the very best. Silk and golden braids. Teenage friends writing poems for him in symbolic candlelight. The wilting marigolds jettisoned for roses—fabulous roses with perfect petals. Kitchen rags used, this time to wipe whiskey from the counter. Butt ends choking up the ashtray. Milk bottles very popular among the ladies for cups of tea.

He reaches the lane, the wind sending stinging raindrops into the side of his face. Cathal can feel the cold seep into his bones as he negotiates the ruts and potholes, using the shovel as a walking stick. In the distance the swans drift on, oblivious to the weather. The strangest thing about it all is that they never seem to quarrel. Yet, then again, they never sing either. Even when they leave, the whole flock, every New Year's Eve, he never hears that swansong. On a television program one night a scientist said that the swan's song was a mythological invention, maybe it had happened once or twice, when a bird was shot in the air, and the escaping breath from the windpipe sounded to some poor foolish poet like a song. But, if it is true, if there is really such a thing as a swansong, wouldn't it be lovely to hear? Cathal whistles through his teeth, then smiles. That way, at least, there'd be no more damn digging and a man could rest.

He unlatches the gate hinge and sidesteps the ooze of mud behind the cattle guard, and tramps on into the field. Water squelches up around his Wellingtons with each step. The birds on the water have not seen him yet. A couple of them follow one another in a line through the water, churning ripples. A large cob, four feet tall, twines his neck with a female, their bills of bright yellow smudged with touches of black. Slowly they reach around and preen each other's feathers. Cathal smiles. There goes Anna Pavlova, his nickname for his favorite swan, a cygnet that, in the early days of the year before the lake became so choc-a-bloc, would dance across the water, sending flumes of spray in the air. Others gather together in the reeds. A group of nine huddle near the bank, their necks stretched out toward the sky.

Bedamned if there's a whole lot of room for another one— especially a boy who's likely to be a bit feisty. Cathal shakes his head and flings the shovel forward to the edge of the lake. It lands blade first and then slides in the mud, almost going into the water. The birds look up and cackle. Some of them start to flap their wings. Wingnut barks.

"Shut up, all of ya," he shouts. "Give a man a break. A bit of peace and quiet."

He retrieves the shovel and wipes the blade on the thigh pocket of his overalls, lights another cigarette, and holds it between his yellowing teeth. Most of the swans settle down, glancing at him. But the older ones who have been there since January turn away and let themselves drift. Wingnut settles on the ground, her head on her front paw. Cathal drives the shovel down hard into the wet soil at the edge of the lake, hoping that he has struck the right spot.

All of them generally shaped, sized, and white-feathered the same. The girl from the blown-up bar looking like a twin of the soldier found slumped in the front seat of a Saracen, a hole in his head the size of a fist, the size of a heart. And him the twin of the boy from Garvagh found drowned in a ditch with an armalite in his fingers and a reed in his teeth. And him the twin of the mother shot accidentally while out walking her baby in a pram. Her the twin of the father found hanging from an oak tree after seeing his daughter in a dress of tar and chicken feathers. Him the twin of the three soldiers and two gunmen who murdered each other last March—Christ, that was some amount of hissing while he dug. And last week, just before Christmas, the old man found on the roadside with his kneecaps missing, beside his blue bicycle, that was a fierce difficult job too.

Now the blade sinks easily. He slams his foot down on the shovel. With a flick of the shoulder and pressure from his feet he lifts the first clod—heavy with water and clumps of grass—flings it to his left, then looks up to the sky, wondering.

Christmas decorations in the barracks perhaps. Tinsel, post-cards, bells, and many bright colors. Pine needles sprayed so they don't fall. A soldier with no stomach for turkey. A soldier ripping into the pudding. Someone chuckling about the mother of all bottles. A boy on a street corner, seeing a patch of deeper black on the tar macadam, making a New Year's resolution. A teacher going through old essays. A girlfriend on an English promenade, smoking. A great-aunt with huge amounts of leftovers. Paragraphs in the bottom left hand corner of newspapers.

Another clodful and the mound rises higher. The rain blows hard into Cathal's back. Clouds scuttle across the morning sky. Cigarette smoke rushes from his nose and mouth. He begins to sweat under all the heavy clothing. After a few minutes he stubs the butt end into the soil, takes out a red handkerchief and wipes his forehead, then pummels at the ground again. Go carefully now, or you'll cut the poor little bastard's delicate neck.

With the mound piled high and the hole three feet deep, Cathal sees the top of a white feather. A tremble of wet soil. "Easy now," he says. "Easy. Don't be thrashing around down there on me." He digs again, a deep wide arc around the swan, then lays the shovel on the ground and spread-eagles himself at the side of the hole. Across the hole he winks at Wingnut, who has seen this happen enough times that she has learned not to bark. On the lake, behind his back, he can hear some of the swans braying. He reaches down into the hole and begins to scrabble at the soil with his fingernails. Why all this sweating in the rain, in a clean white shirt, when there's a million and one other things to be done? The clay builds up deep in his fingernails. The bird is sideways in the soil.

He reaches down and around the body and loosens the dirt some more, but not enough for the wings to start flapping. One strong blow of those things could break a man's arm. He lays his hands on the stomach and feels the heart flutter. Then he scrabbles some more dirt from around the webbed feet. With great delicacy Cathal makes a tunnel out of which to pull the neck and head. With the soil loose enough he gently eases the long twisted neck out and grabs it with one hand. "Don't be hissing there now." He slips his other hand in around the body. Deftly he lifts the swan out of the soil, folding back one of the feet against the wing, keeping the other wing close to his chest. He lifts the swan into the air, then throws it away from him.

"Go on now, you little upstart."

Cathal sits on the edge of the hole with his Wellington boots dangling down and watches the wondrous way that the swan bursts over the lake, soil sifting off its wings, curious and lovely, looking for a place to land. He watches as the other swans make room by sliding in, crunching against one another's wings. The newborn settles down on a small patch of water on the eastern side of the lake.

Somewhere in the bowels of a housing complex, a mother is packing away clothes in black plastic bags. Her lip quivers. There's new graffiti on the stairwell wall down from her flat. Pictures of footballers are coming down off a bedroom wall. A sewing needle is flung into an empty dustbin where it rattles. Outside, newspapermen use shorthand in little spiral books. Cameras run on battery packs. Someone thinks of putting some sugar in the water so that the flowers will last longer. Another man, in a flat cap, digs. A soldier is dialing his girlfriend. Or carving a notch. Swans don't sing unless they're shot way up high, up there, in the air. Their windpipes whistle. That's a known fact.

Cathal lights his last cigarette and thinks about how, in two days, the whole flock will leave and the digging may well have to begin all over again. Well, fuck it all anyway. Every man has his own peculiar curse. Cathal motions to his dog, lifts his shovel, then leans home toward the farmhouse in his green boots. As he walks, splatters of mud leap up on the back of his anorak. The smoke blows away in spirals from his mouth. He notices how the fencepost in the far corner of the field is leaning a little drunkenly. That will have to be fixed, he thinks, as the rain spits down in flurries.

Made in the USA
Lexington, KY
21 February 2011